Said the Crow

A Gothic Novella

Ellen Taylor

For Joe

This story was inspired by the events of the Spring 2020 lockdown – both real and imagined.

I
EXODUS

When we arrive at the cottage, the landlord is already there. His jeep is sitting in the driveway, and he leans against its bonnet. It only occurs to me now that we could have asked him for a lift from the station.

Instead, we asked my father to take the train across from Edinburgh to Glasgow, then hire a removal van to drive us some hundred miles north, through the Monadhliath mountain pass and into the flat, barren country. It was a long drive, and we are weary from it. But we're here now, and that's all that matters.

The landlord leans across the wall, which is made of grey slabbed stone. In deep winter (I know from the agency portfolio) moss will grow on the crown of that wall, shrouding it in a cloak of green. Thorns of holly will creep through the black gaps in the stone. Now, it is spring. The landlord glances up from under his cap as I click the passenger door open. He wears green Wellington boots and a tattered tweed jacket to match. Like a deer stalker, I think. He stubs out his cigarette on the wall and lets its butt drop, lost amongst the leaf-scabbed hedge. An arm extends.

"You must be Rosie." His accent is thick and gruff-sounding. I recognise it from our conversation on the phone.

"Nice to finally meet you," I say, taking his hand.

He has a firm grip. Strong, solid hands. They are somehow more real than the journey here has been: the landscape streaming past in a blur of yellow-green; elusive, ungraspable. He nods to me, and then to Mark who wavers at my side. "Want me to show you inside?"

I glance back to my father, but he is preoccupied with his roadmap, perhaps trying to find a faster route home.

Back to the landlord. "That would be good. Thanks."

We follow him through the latched gate, down the cobbled path to the slate-painted door. This too I have meticulously studied, and I know exactly where the paint is beginning to peel; exactly how the knocker stares, its eyes two blank spaces carved into steel, the handle secured like a gag to its mouth.

Mark nudges me nervously, prompting me to raise what we discussed this morning in the flat. I clear my throat.

But when the words come out, I baulk.

"What is the energy efficiency rating?" I ask instead.

The landlord starts talking about smart meters and about having someone come to fit the double glazing. But I'm not really listening. My eyes are on Mark, who stares at his foot, tapping against the chipped patio. This is not the question he wanted me to ask.

We are through the gate when I summon the courage to try again.

"The agency mentioned..." I stop and start over. "They mentioned we can walk to town through the woods. Is it a long way?"

4

He's giving us directions now. Straight through the trees along the track. *Keep to the path*, he says. Mark is giving me a sideways glance. He wants to know, but he won't ask himself. I can't expect him to.

I swallow and ask:

"The agency mentioned there was an accident here. We just wanted to know a bit more about what happened?"

At first, I think he looks angry. But then the landlord gives a wry smile.

"Accident is a funny way of putting it," he says dryly. "Though there's nothing wrong with the house itself, if that's what you're worried about. Living out here... It's not for everyone."

He seems reluctant to say more, but my nerves are eased. The solitude will be good for us. I know it will.

The landlord is about to turn the key in the lock when, beside me, I feel Mark stiffen. He's staring up at the window above us. It's a pretty frame made of weathered wood. Outside, there's a rose bush that jitters gently against the glass. On it are three single flowers. The rest is thorn. I put my arm around Mark, and he looks at me. His eyes are bewildered, almost mournful. Then he forces a smile that makes me melt. This must be so hard for him.

The landlord leads us through the rooms, displaying them one by one. Vaguely, he points out features that might be of interest – the Victorian fireplace, the new internet router that winks in a conspiratorial flash of red. We listen politely, knowing that it wouldn't make a difference if the house were a wreck and the walls caked in mould. We have paid the deposit. There's no going back now.

"Any questions?" the landlord asks when he's done.

I raise my shoulders in a shrug. Look to Mark; nothing.

"I think you've covered everything. Thank you."

"That your van? The one you came here in?"

"We hired it."

He looks us up and down. Sizing Mark up, it feels like. Maybe he wonders what's wrong with him. Then he pulls another cigarette from his pocket and holds it between his lips, dry.

"Your car on its way?"

"I don't drive," I say.

His eyebrows raise, and the cigarette jerks slightly in his mouth. A quick glance to Mark, but then he thinks better of it. His hands continue to fumble for a lighter.

"We like walking," I say brightly. A desperate attempt to compensate. I feel like a schoolgirl, found scratching her name into the wood of a desk. A child denied her sweeties. *Please don't take this away from me.*

My enthusiasm is maybe too much. He sucks on his cigarette as if it's alight. He gives something of a shrug, turning away from us. Beside me, Mark says nothing.

In the kitchen, the landlord clicks his lighter. He stands halfway between the inside and out, breathing in chugs. The agency said no smoking

6

was permitted on the premises. But I can't say anything: this is his house.

"Will be a pain walking about when the snow sets in."

It's strange, hearing the word snow now. Though the air is still chill, we have already shrugged off the worst of winter. Buds sprout in the hedgerows. The days grow longer, the sun finally biting away the shroud of eternal night. From the elm tree at the end of the garden, birds sing.

The snow will come, I don't deny it. But we're not so far out that we can't get groceries delivered. I already checked the postcode. The biting, barren landscape we passed on the mountain road seems an age away from us now. I smile, politely, waiting for him to give us the keys.

He flicks his cigarette out the door. Ash falls across the threshold. I can feel Mark looking at it. The residue grows larger the longer he stares.

Back to the landlord. He gives a brusque cough. Looks me up and down with one swift glance.

"You not working, then?"

"Remotely," I say.

He scratches his ear, thinking for something else to say. "Well. Any problems, you've got my phone number."

"Yes," I say, filled with relief.

He glances at Mark again. I wonder what he's thinking. *What's a pretty girl like you doing with a boy like him?* Then he holds out the key and drops it in my hands.

I feel it in my palm. The weight of it, solid iron. It's jagged with possibility; of doors opened, of secrets unlocked. I feel like Pandora, unfastening her box.

My fingers close around the key and foolishly I think, *I'm home.*

We're standing in the kitchen, the boxes dismantled and lying flat against the table chairs. We've unpacked most of the downstairs, with just our clothes and the bathroom items to sort through tonight. Dad helped with the heavy lifting before stretching deliberately and stifling a mock yawn.

"Right kids, that's me all done. I better hit the road before it gets dark."

He calls us kids even though we're not. Then he gives Mark a wink, as though his words hide some cryptic code that only the male brain can decipher. Mark is kind enough to smile in return.

"You're sure you don't want another tea, Dad?"

"No lass, best not."

He hovers there for a second, unsure of himself. The skin around his eyes pinches together. For one horrific moment, I think he might cry. He's done it before, at my graduation, and then again two years ago as he walked me down the aisle. *Please don't*, I will him. *Please. Not now.*

Then at last he breaks into a smile. There's pride in that smile, I think, and it reassures me. This is the right decision, after all, determined

8

by the most reliable source. We move forwards to the doorway, watching him as he waddles down the cobbled path.

"Take care of her, won't you?" he says to Mark before disappearing into his van.

The irony is not lost on us.

Now we are alone. Three mugs sit on the drying board. A splash of milk is left on the tabletop. I look around the room and marvel at what is now my home. The counters are made of painted wood. You can still see the knots where branches were once born, morphed into shapeless faces: the skewed hook of a nose, the almond rings of an eye.

Everything in this house has been chosen deliberately. The Aga 60 with its single hob; the sturdy pine tabletop, worn down with scuffs like an old chopping board. There's a porcelain vase on the windowsill – empty – and a shelf fitted above the hanging pans where recipe books are collecting dust. On the wall is an antique clockface, with its second-hand slowly ticking by. In the next room, there's a fireplace, built like an altar into the wall. Two sofas sit solemnly, cushions bowed in prayer, their floral fabric humbled with the nibbling bites of moth. There's a writing desk in the corner, and a stiff wooden chair that now holds the weight of boxes to be unpacked. Upstairs, less explored: a cramped room with one iron-framed double and a mahogany wardrobe pressed up against the wall; one bathroom containing just that – a bath – and a separate toilet closet at the end of the corridor.

It's so different from our old flat, which seemed to be pieced together from spare parts. The door's lock had been fitted upside down there, so that each time I let myself in or out, the keys would bash against the metal ungivingly: a daily resistance, gnashing like teeth. Somehow I never remembered this, despite the months we lived there. Each evening I would twist the key the wrong way, then have to double back: two flicks of the wrist, as grievous as turning back time.

Time. The digits on our old oven that I'd somehow set to 12:15. I must have thought it was a clock, then forgotten how to change it. It started when the oven turned on, so that each tray of chicken nuggets would be ready at 12:35; each casserole cooked for approximately 13:00. A life of lunchtimes, even when the working day was done.

There were three switches in the kitchen-diner of our old apartment, corresponding to the three lightbulbs screwed into the ceiling above. There was no logical order between them. The first switch would turn on the middle light, the middle the last, and the last the first – or was it another way round? I never mastered the lights either. On some level, I always knew our life there was temporary. A station waiting room when the train is delayed. Long but finite.

This house is much better. It's old, sure, and it's not much bigger than our flat. The paint is peeling and the doors creaks from the stiff wood. But there's a cohesiveness here that feels like an exhale. I think of rocks at the bottom of a river, smoothed soft by the rush of water. This house has been carved by time, cut out of it, set apart for us to enjoy. It feels like a secret. *Our* secret. Our sanctuary.

The floor is stone, worn down around the table like a forest path. There are glass jars at the back of the counters with metal pop clasps. In the agency photos, the jars were filled with pasta and tea leaves and each one plastered with a hand-scribed label. Those labels have been peeled off now, but I can still see the white scrapes left behind, clinging like frost in the shadows of a winter morning. Like ghosts who have not yet turned their back on life.

Everything in this kitchen could be plucked from another age. We stand here to witness it – time travellers from the future. And our microwave, sitting conspicuously on the kitchen table, is our spaceship. Soon it will zap us up into a frenzy of atoms and whizz us away.

I look at Mark, eager to share with him this image. It's just the kind of stilted, geeky humour that he loves. But he's not looking at me. He's staring about the room with a strange expression. His face is clouded somehow. Watchful. He looks as though he's trying to work out how we got here – like a sleepwalker who has just woken up.

When dinnertime comes, we cook our meals in the microwave. Two beef lasagnes, bought chilled from a petrol station forty miles away. We sit on the sofas beside the fire that isn't lit, with the garish light from the table lamp casting shadows across us.

"I feel tired," Mark says.

"We'll go up to bed soon."

"We need to finish unpacking the boxes."

"It can wait until morning."

I've dropped a piece of beef from my ready meal. I put the plastic tray on the sofa and bend down to find it. It's a different world down here, full of loose fibres from the carpet and the odd splotches of dirt. Did we make those, clumsily trailing in mud from our shoes? Or were they here already? My hand reaches out. My fingers stretch to where I can't see. They slide over something bony and soft. A feather?

I can't find the piece of beef. I picture it, growing mould like a rock grows crystal. I imagine it stinking, decaying, like a corpse.

Blood rushes to my head. A woozy tingling fills me; pins and needles, like the sea heard from the hollow of a shell. I draw myself up, feeling cold and faint. The beef will have to rot there. I look at Mark, hoping that he hasn't noticed.

He's not looking at me. His eyes are wandering, unseeing, across the mantle of the fireplace. His gaze grasps hold of things – the crack in the wall's plaster; the tilt of the oil painting that hangs at my back – then lets them slip away. The cold in my head has spread to my fingertips now. It prickles at my spine. At times like this, I wonder if I am just a crack in the wall plaster, a tilt of a painting. Does he really see me?

"Mark."

12

He looks back at me. The shiver intensifies – electric – and then it's gone.

"I'm sorry," he says, looking down at his hands. "I'm sorry."

"Hush. What are you sorry for?"

There are many answers he could give, but instead he chooses silence. I move onto his sofa with him, ready meal forgotten.

"It's okay," I tell him. "It's all going to be okay."

We sit like that for maybe an hour before we finally decide to go to bed. The duvet covers are dressed in dusty pink overalls, with the print of flowers tangled around the hem. I'm eager to climb straight between them and sleep, but I can see Mark staring the bed down nervously, eying the reddish stain that has seeped into the fabric at the far side. So I find our own covers from our boxes (cotton; freshly laundered) and get to work changing the sheets.

"What side do you want?" I ask him.

"I don't mind."

"Well you pick, and I'll squeeze in beside you."

He picks the side against the wall and curls up there. It's dark outside. I can see the moon in glimpses, caught between cloud and thorn. The thorn comes from the rose bush, the one I noticed earlier, which has grown thick against the grass. A single, blushing bud hangs limply from its branch to tap against the window. *Tap, tap, tap.* Like the beating wings of a bird.

I decide to leave the curtains open. No-one will see us here in the country, and I've always struggled to sleep in the pitch black. I expect Mark to say something. He was always funny about the curtains in our old flat: drawing them as soon as it was dark and pulling them open each morning before breakfast. But he's curled up tight away from me. Maybe he's already asleep.

I lie in the half-darkness, thinking of the life that stretches ahead. It's so quiet here, so different to the hum of the city. It hardly feels real. We have entered a tangential universe: a muted world, under water, upside down, carved out from the hollow of the bloated stomach where we once lived.

Tomorrow we'll explore the garden. I want to plant a vegetable patch when the weather warms up. We have a south-facing wall with a plot beneath it: perfect for tomatoes and gooseberries and runner-beans, so long as we remember to cover them before the frost sets in. We can walk to the lake, too, and see if we can swim there. The agency website claimed we could.

I'm excited to live by the woodland. It's not large enough to be called a forest – not up here, where those things have meaning; where a mountain is a monolith, not simply a hill. But it's big enough to get lost in: an acre at least of dense trees. In autumn, we can go searching for mushrooms. I've always wanted to search for mushrooms. To know odd facts about them; to sort into piles of which will be cooked and which

14

will be dried; and which — thin and deadly — might make us convulse, and fit, and die.

I remember what the landlord said about snow. I imagine it with child-like wonder. A carpet of white; pure and virginal. Not like the yellowing sludge of the city. When winter draws in the darkness, we'll light a fire downstairs. I'll make cocoa on the Aga and serve it in thick, ceramic mugs. We'll laze around on the sofas; me with my laptop, Mark with a book. Maybe he's better by then. Maybe my stomach is swelling, my cheeks rosy with the glow of new life...

But let's not get ahead of ourselves.

I stare at the ceiling, feeling the springs of the mattress beneath me. A firm bed. Good for the back. The moonlight washes over us like an ocean. I think of faraway waters. Of tides, wrapping their way around our ankles and cradling us in their arms.

I breathe out and watch the air unmoving above me. I wonder who else has breathed this air. Who else lay here before us, skin some inches apart, letting their breath tangle together like smoke? The thought is comforting.

Mark is hunched over beside me. From his breathing, I think he's asleep. I curl into him, like a flower wilting at sundown. My stomach presses against his back. My knees knock against his thighs. I think of myself as a tree, rooting. I think (and if you think really hard, thoughts can come true) that things will start to get better, now.

A foolish notion, yet look at us. We are here.

We wake in the morning to a blissful silence. Mark rolls onto his side beside me and smiles.

"Good morning," he says.

"Good morning."

We stay in bed, enjoying a languid half-hour of laziness, then get up to brush our teeth. I turn on the taps and splash my face. The water is cold and icy. It feels like the crest of a wave.

The plan had been to go to the sea.

Sea air, they used to say. *It'll be good for you. Fresh air and salt inside your lungs.*

I'd imagined a stony cottage by the shore. A secret cove, maybe hidden by cliffs, or just a white strip of sand beyond the dunes. I saw us scrambling over rockpools, knees scraped, salt in the wounds. We would collect shells as though they were treasure and line them up in a procession along our garden wall. Maybe we'd fill our bathroom with them: shelves and nooks brimming with limpets and cockles and whelks. A bathtub filled with kelp.

We would breathe the sea like a tonic. Gin and tonic; the poor man's drink. Holy water. Vitamin Sea.

Take your pills and you'll feel better soon.

We couldn't afford a cottage near the coast. Not on my salary alone. Lochside was also out of the question, and any of the picturesque highland towns. The best I could find was this cottage, beautiful if isolated, two miles from the nearest village. But it's not all bad, being inland. We're further from the rush of the traffic here. Tourist seasons won't touch us, nor will pesky neighbours, nosy for gossip, sniffing it out like

16

badgers in bins. There's a lochan a short hike away, and the woods to walk through. If we try, very hard, I think that we could be happy here.

At my side, Mark is struggling to breathe properly. He does a good job of hiding it, but I can see it in his posture. The way his shoulders bunch up tight. The shivering of his Adam's apple, straining as he clenches his jaw. The act is for my benefit. Or maybe it's for himself. He stares at his reflection in the mirror, eyes bulging, a tremor catching his lips in a twitch. I stand next to him and lace my fingers between his. Then, reaching forwards, I open the bathroom cabinet. The reflection sways away from us, lost. I unscrew the caps of the prescription bottles that sit there. Duloxetine, Propranolol, Seroquel. Strange names from a strange world that now know how to roll off our tongues.

"Take your pills," I tell him, passing him the bottle.

You'll feel better soon.

I told the psychiatrist that I would call when we had settled in. There is a special procedure for transferring clients between branches. Even without yesterday's journey, you'd know we are long way from Glasgow here. Another country altogether, it feels. The psychiatrist will talk me through this over the phone.

I make the call from the lane. The signal is bad in the cottage, and the landline hasn't yet been wired up. I knew there'd be a delay when we first contacted the agency. *The wires have been cut*, they said. Something to do with the accident. I remember it very clearly because the choice of words seemed strange. *Cut.* Implying that it was deliberate. That the damage was man-made.

The path is thick with mud, caked stubbornly against shallow puddles, refusing to dry despite the sun. The hedgerows lining the track are bare, but florets of wintry blossom are beginning to bud in patches.

Phone to ear, I listen to the dial tone.

Hello, we're a little busy right now. Please hold the line.

A thrush cocks its head as I pass. A breeze makes the blossom buds shiver, sprinkling a few lone petals onto my path. The same sounds, in my ear, a hundred miles away from our old flat. The same piano music, interspersed with the mild Glaswegian voice – *Did you know that you can book appointments online via our website?* – as though I am still pacing up and down the box-like apartment, Mark on the sofa, head in hands, rocking – still squeezing his hand as his nails dig into my flesh – still –

"Good morning, Dr Vogel's office?"

I'm turning off the lane, onto the footpath. The trail skirts the ring of woodland, trees on one side, a ditch on the other. Beyond are farmland fields, now bare of crop, chopped down to tufts of grass. How nice it will look in summer, I think.

"Hi, this is Rosie Graham. The doctor said that if I rang this morning I'd be put through?"

A shuffling of paper, on the other side. I can hear a car going past in the street. I think how, only weeks ago, I stood on that street. How Mark was sweating. How I had to drag him inside.

I cross a bridge over the ditch, reaching the open farmland. I follow the verges, hearing the squelch of boots in the mud. The phone clicks. I've been put through.

"Rosie. What can I do for you? Are you all settled in?"

"We moved yesterday," I tell him.

"How did that go?"

It is classic Vogel. There is no jumping to the point. We could chat like this for half an hour before getting down to business.

I am in no rush.

I tell him about the cottage. The chipped white paint that I can still see now, far across the fields. I tell him the way the walls are swallowed by rose creepers; the three single flowers, so light and pink that the petals look like fingertips, standing defiant against the thawing winter winds. I tell him about the sprouts of hollyhock-stems in the garden, and how there'll be flowers soon, burgeoning, reaching for the skies. I tell him about Mark; how he stood in the kitchen staring around him; how he realised that we were finally home.

"It sounds as though things are good."

Good. What a glorious understatement. The sun is beating down from the midmorning sky. The birds ahead singing. It's not warm, but there is the breath of spring in the air – the promise of longer days ahead. Wisps of cloud float overhead;

19

the wind whistles as it catches the trees. Soon, daisies will sprout from the undergrowth, and hemlock will grow unruly at my sides. There's a sycamore ahead, already budding with new leaves, standing tall and stoic between the borders of field. If the grass is dry enough, I might sit there a while.

Yes, I tell him, things are good.

He's talking about medication now. Asking how much we have left – how often it's being taken. Have you registered with a doctor yet? He asks.

No, but it's next on my list of things to do.

He begins to talk about numbers I can call – services outside of the city. I should have taken a pen, I realise. I try to remember the names, strange pseudonyms, coded like superheroes. *Night support. The watchline.* The sycamore is above me, its shadow passing over my face. That's when the sound cuts in.

SSSSSSSCCCCCCHHHHHH

It's so loud my ears feel like they're bleeding. Bold and incessant. Without end. I pull the phone away from my ear, cringing back from the white noise. I scan the fields in panic, the empty plains, our white cottage half-hidden from view. Something has jumped into the telephone – into my brain. An alien intervention. I am exposed and alone.

And then it stops.

A crackling of static. A broken voice. "Rosie? Are you still there?"

I look up to the sky, as if searching for explanation. The clouds are still wispy and thin. The sun beats cold.

Did you hear that?

"Hear what?" Dr Vogel asks.

"That noise."

I hold the phone some inches away, ears pricked. The air is alert. It's listening to me.

There's something watching. I can feel its eyes on me: a sixth sense. I turn in a crescent, then back on myself again. I expect a farmer, a deer, a hare on its hind legs. But there is nothing. Just the empty wind and the sound of cawing birds overhead. Dampened with the distance, I hear Vogel clear his throat. "I think there might be something wrong with your connection."

Carefully, I lift the phone back to my ear. I can hear my breathing – or his. Mine reflected through his. The grass fields are still. The air holds its breath. Then:

"Hello?"

"Hello," I say. I've turned around now, marching back to the cottage. Specs of mud fly up from my boots, crusting the hem of my jeans. "Sorry. The signal's bad here."

"Ah. I can hear you now. I was just saying, that if you need more medication before the prescription comes through..."

The wind rustles. I wish I'd worn a jacket. A cardigan seemed enough on spring days in Glasgow, the tall buildings blocking out the cold, the walk from the flat to the corner shop, the corner shop to the bus stop, the bus stop to the office, never more than five minutes if you're brisk about it. But here the fields are wild and bare. There's nothing to break the wind except the woodland, now some hundred yards behind me.

Dr Vogel continues to talk. There seem a million things to remember. I break them down into compartments in my head, a technique I've been practising. Make molehills out of mountains. The medication, the GP surgery, the pharmacy. A wind whips through the air, making the grass bow in submission. It reminds me of a gale across a loch, bending water in its wake. I think of the lake in the hills, only an hour's walk away. A lochan in a valley, surrounded by a ring of trees. I wonder if the water is warm enough for swimming.

I'm getting distracted.

I need to focus. For Mark. It's my job to take care of him. God knows what he'd do without me. I need to listen to every word that the doctor is saying, hold it in my head, remember it. I will his words to etch themselves into my skull.

"And remember," Vogel is saying now, "if things get bad again, if you don't know where else to turn, you can call me. I'm only a phone call away."

"Yes," I say. Yes, thank you. I'll be sure to give you a call. Yes, Dr Vogel, it's lovely here. Thank you for your help. Talk soon.

I hang up, my empty farewell reverberating in my head. *Talk soon*, I told him, well aware that we might never speak again.

Today we will go to the village to shop. It's quite a walk through the woodland, but I'm eager to try the route. We have a delivery coming tomorrow with all the essentials, plus our bag of service-station gems. But it would be nice to have some fresh vegetables to cook with tonight, and some more milk for our tea in the morning. I'm excited to see what they have.

Mark doesn't want to come to the village. He hasn't told me that exactly, but I can see it in the way he moves, sluggishly, going through the motions of getting dressed while holding onto the hope that he won't have to. That I'll turn around and tell him it's alright; he can stay here. That he shouldn't do too much; maybe he should run himself a nice, warm bath.

Instead, I smile at him. "You're not going to make me walk there on my own, are you?"

It's in this gentle voice that I make him believe he's doing me a favour. That he can still look after me, the way that I look after him.

We squeeze our feet into our walking boots by the door. Mine are from a charity shop on Argyle Street. I couldn't afford them new and they're half a size too small. Mark's were a gift last Christmas.

Out the door and into the open. You can feel a freshness here that's different to the city. It's not just the smell of the country, but the weight of it. Things are lighter here.

"It's a nice day," Mark says, looking up to the sky. The clouds have become glorious, thick and white and catching the sun like gold.

I beam at him, my mind full of summer. "Yes. It is."

We walk together along the track, away from the cottage. When I look back on the sheltered garden, I feel the small sense of pride seeded in my stomach begin to take shape. From here we can only see one side of the house: the stone side, at the back, with the rose bush climbing up to our bedroom window.

We talk about what we'll buy from the shop. Mark is dreaming of Scotch eggs and bacon. I tell him that we have bacon coming in the delivery tomorrow, so there's no need to buy more of that – but maybe it will be fresher if we buy it local. Maybe we should treat ourselves, now that we've come this far.

We talk about the cottage, too. This is of more interest to me than it is to Mark. I want to know where we're putting the atlas and the textbooks Mark still has from his degree. Really, I think we should throw them out, they only make for clutter, but this isn't a popular opinion with Mark. He says that he'll feel lost without them. Oh please can't we just keep them, he says. And I think, why not? If it makes him happy, then we can stack them under the desk, or lean them on the windowsill upstairs. They'll serve as an amulet: an evil eye disguised as *An Introduction to Economics.* Their blockish presence is a small price to pay for the peace they will bring.

We trace the path uphill and into the woodland. The trees are uniform silver pines. They must have been planted in the past century, because though they're tall and thin, their lines are too straight to be a natural occurrence. The trees here have been planted like crops. Each one stands four or five metres from its vertical neighbour, and there's a gap of ten to twelve metres before the next stripe. And there are rows of them: row after row after row. When we look down each line, it's straight as an arrow. Then, as we move further away, the shapes bent and skew like diamonds. They warp like a mirror, fish-eyed. A piney kaleidoscope, dancing just for us.

My hands find Mark's. Our arms swing together like a metronome. I can feel him staring into the trees, untrusting. It's my job to distract him. I swing my arm higher. My grip on his fingers tightens.

We skirt ditches and thicket as we follow the dirt track to the village. Occasionally, an arm shoots off from the trail: a sandy limb reaching out to farm or wasteland. The land we're on is private. Only this bridleway belongs to us. It brings to mind old wives' tales and fables: *don't stray too far from the path.*

The chatter is thinning between us. I've already said all there is to say about the cottage, talking through each room in turn; listing the things I want to grow in the garden, and what needs cutting back, and how we'll get it done before the summer comes to an end. "Did you hear the rose last night, tapping against the window? I bet the bush looks beautiful in bloom..."

Mark has stopped. He's staring down one of the arms that reaches through the forest. This track is almost as wide as the one we're walking on. The rows of trees don't quite reach its edges. There's a border of cowslip and nettles growing there instead. Like the white margin on the sides of a book.

I tug at Mark's arm to pull him away. But he's like a dog who has seen a rabbit. He doesn't budge. Then I follow his eyes, down the track that cuts through the trees, and I frown. There's something there. A box, on the side of the road.

"What is it?" Mark says.

Slowly, I pull my hand out from between his. My palms feel clammy all of a sudden. I wipe them on my jeans.

"I'm not sure."

His ears are pricked like a dog's too. He's alert to everything. A rustle comes from the pines beside us; a deer or a rabbit, chased away by the sound of our voice. Mark tenses as it moves. His spine is so tight that I can feel its strain. It's like the air bends around it, yielding to a force stiffer than the gravity that pins us down.

"Can we see it?" he asks.

I want to say no. I want to get to the village and find the shop. Get our things and get back home. But there's no way I can think to say this without disappointing him. What excuse can I give? So I say, "Okay."

We turn off the main path and down the arm of track. This is private land now, but you wouldn't know it. The trees look the same here as they did from the bridleway: lines and diamonds, curving for us as we pass. My shoes are caked in a layer of dust. Funny, I could have sworn it was muddy before. But here, the track is so dry, the earth feels thirsty. The dust makes a thin haze for us to walk through. The ground is exhaling with our every step.

The box grows closer. Or rather, we grow closer to it. I can see now that it's not a box at all. It's a cage.

The cage is thin and short. Its bars are dense, not in squares exactly, but rectangles that follow from top to bottom, and side to side at regular intervals. You could swipe a credit card through those bars, I think, only catching the metal on its very sides. You could poke your finger in there – just the tip of it, before the knuckle – and run it through the jaws of the cage as though feeling the bars for dust.

You could, but you wouldn't want to. You wouldn't want to because of what's inside.

There's a bird in there. I could barely recognise it from afar. It was just a mass of black, half-hidden by the bars. But now I can see quite clearly. I think: the bird is a blackbird, only it's bigger. I think: maybe it's a crow.

It's trapped inside the cage.

On top of the prison is a piece of fibreboard. The board has been slotted through the bars to shelter it from the sunlight. To provide shade, perhaps, or to seal it shut? Maybe that's what is trapping the bird there. I wonder who has done this.

"I don't like it," Mark says from beside me. He's scratching his arm as though there's a rash there I cannot see. "Why's it in there? Can you get it out?"

I turn back to the bird. It's cramped. There's not enough room for it in the cage. Its feathers are damaged on its right wing, as though it panicked and flapped against the metal bars. Did they put it in here because it's injured? There's a water drip fixed to the outside of the rails. The kind you'd find on a rabbit hutch, feeding water drop by drop like a syringe. But the liquid inside looks too yellow to be water. I wonder if it's medicine. Maybe that's why they put it here. They want to keep it safe until it's better. There are a few bits of corn on the ground beside it. Mark keeps scratching his arms. The bird in the cage flaps.

"Can't you do something?" Mark cries. "Can't you get it out?!"

"Calm down," I tell him. "It must be here for a reason. Let me see what I can do..."

I bend down in front of the cage to investigate. It's been put here to heal, that must be it. The water and the food mean it can't be a mistake. But why is the cage so small, if it's for the bird's safety? It can barely stretch its wings out, let alone move around.

I squat in front of it, searching for a way to open the box up.

The trap is made of three compartments. I open one side and find a diagonal wall that lifts when I pull it apart. There's a hook on the top bars, and I realise I can latch this door open. I do so, moving the cage carefully so that I don't startle the bird inside. The crow gives a mild squawk, as though questioning my intentions.

The door is now open. I reach my hand inside to the next component – the centre cage where the crow now sits. I can see that the other side is identical: a rising door with a latch it attaches to. But the mid-section is a puzzle, a riddle that I cannot solve. I look up at Mark. His face is white as a sheet. Then I scan our surroundings, feeling like a child with their hand stuck in a cookie jar. *We shouldn't be here.*

On the side of the road beside us, half swallowed by nettles, is a drum. It's big. It would nearly reach my waist if I were to stand next to it. And at the bottom of the drum are some pellets, just like the ones in the cage. Corn and millet and blinking eyes of sunflower seeds. *For feeding pheasants*, I think vaguely, remembering the farmland we used to visit near my aunt and uncle's place. Feed them up and shoot them down. A good hunting season will bring in twice as much as a field of crop.

The bird squawks again, as if I've forgotten it. Its bent feathers hang limply. It blinks at me. It's a prisoner. A real-life scarecrow, serving as a warning to its friends. An example made. A head on a spike.

"*Mark*," the bird caws suddenly. It looks at me. I peer at it, trying to figure out whether I heard it right. Then it screeches again. "*Mark.*"

Perhaps it's just my imagination. We've been walking a long time, and I'm tired. But then I remember Poe's raven; its sombre nevermore. Crows and rooks and other clever birds... They

29

mimic speech like parrots. It must have heard me saying Mark's name, and it's echoing it back! Smart creature. I lean forwards to touch its beak.

The bird flaps its wings and cries.

"Mark!" It screams.

"Rosie..." Mark warns from behind me.

"It's okay, Mark. I just need to figure out..."

I bite my cheek. My hand moves forward. My wrist presses down as I manoeuvre my fingers. It brushes against the ground and *snap!*

"Fuck!" I shout. The trap has closed on me. I yank my hand away and the cage rattles as I try to free myself. The crow begins to shriek.

Mark is gasping for breath. I can see the panic in his eyes as he stares at me. "I want to go home," he tells himself, scratching his arm. "I want to go home." A mantra. His eyes are beginning to leak.

I pull my arm from the cage. No good. The crow tumbles this way and that, struggling to pick itself up. Its water is splashing. Blotches of yellow stain the newspaper lining. The corn is lost through the silver bars. I see the bird's head bash against the side. A wing caught on metal. Mark is hissing beside me. I can hear the skin being scraped off his arm. I wish he would stop scratching. I wish he would shut up.

I squeeze my eyes shut. *Breathe,* I tell myself. *You have to remember to breathe.* I block out the flapping of the crow, its wings whipping cold air against my palm. I shut out Mark's hyperventilating too. *Breathe, and pick up the door with your other hand.*

Carefully, I attach the trap back to its hook. I slide my hand out, then stare again at the puzzle. Two white cable ties are attached to the bars. I think at first that they must be tied to an entrance, but when I slide them along, I realise they're pointless. A decoy, to stop me from disarming the bomb.

I turn to the fibreboard instead. It's wedged between two parts of the cage, arching slightly where it's bent to fit. I try to move it, but it's stuck. The cage rattles again, and the bird flaps in protest. I stop and take a breath. "It's okay," I mutter out loud. "I'm trying to help you."

One hand must hold the cage in place. This is necessary if I don't want the bird to get hurt. But it means I have to move the fibreboard with my remaining hand alone. It's a struggle; the thing is tucked in tight. The wood is cracking at its centreline. I shuffle it this way and that, slowly coaxing it out. Eventually one side comes loose, and the rest is easy. I pull the thing out and push it to the side.

The bird blinks up at me. It's curious now. No longer afraid. Here is the opening, at the top of the cage. My fingers dig in between the bars to grasp it. I hold the bird's stare, trusting it not to peck at my fingers. It continues to blink.

The cage is open. I reach inside for the bird, but it backs away. My hands go to scoop its body, but the opening is too small. I can't move my wrist properly. The bird flaps again, battering its wings against the cage. It would be impossible to get it out without hurting the poor thing. I don't even know if it will fit.

I take my hand out. I stand up. My thighs ache dully from squatting.

"What are you doing?" Mark says. "We have to get it out of there!"

"We can't," I tell him. "Not without injuring it. But it has a clear exit now. If we leave it here, it will find its way out of the cage."

Mark looks at me in horror. He doesn't believe me, that's for sure. But I am the rational one here. I must make the decisions. I cannot give in to emotion, or all we have built will surely fall apart.

I stare at the bird. My mouth is set in a hard line. Grim, I think I look. I take a step back to give it space.

The crow blinks at me, then it cocks its head and looks up. Another step back. It's looking my way.

We wait there, holding our breath. I can feel the nerves around Mark, electric. They're coiling in my stomach too. *Run*, the wind whispers. *Get out of here, while there's still a chance.* Steadily, we watch the bird.

The crow hops a step to the right. It pecks down at the newspaper at a blotch where its water had spilt. It finds nothing, and pecks again. It stares at us, unblinking now, as we slowly back away.

"Why doesn't it try to escape?" Mark asks from beside me. I can feel his breath, hot against my cheek. His arms are trembling, and I loop mine through his.

"I don't know," I tell him. "Come on. Let's go."

Mark is still shaking when we reach the village. I have to tell him that there's nothing else we could have done. If we'd pushed the cage over, its water could have spilt, leaving it with nothing to drink. If we'd tried to pull it out, we could have damaged its wings beyond repair. "We'll check it on the way back," I tell him as we finally reach the end of woodland. "If it hasn't made its own way out, we'll call the SSPCA."

He doesn't seem convinced, but he doesn't say anything. I can see the trails of red along his arms where he's been scratching. In some places the skin has broken, just slightly, so that small pricks of blood are beginning to gather in beads. He sees me looking and he tries to cover it with his hand. I take his other and we continue to walk.

The village is smaller than I'd expected. There are quite a few houses, but not huddled together in the way you'd expect from a settlement. The buildings are dotted around with no real thought or structure. A cottage here. A farmhouse there. Some of the houses are old, like ours. Others look as though they're made of grey cement, harsh and imposing.

We walk downhill where the path joins up with the road. That road will link back with the one near our house eventually, but the walk through the woods cuts off some miles.

We find the shop. There are two: a farmer's outlet selling strings of meat and fresh vegetables, and a Londis. We hover for a while outside the farmer's outlet, staring into the glass cabinet at the rows of pies and slabs of cheese. There are florescent stars cut from cardboard stuck to the various meats. *2-4-1* the card tells us in orange and pink. *Buy local – special offer.*

"It will be cheaper in Londis," I say. So that's where we go.

I decide I'll make a pie of my own. We have pastry arriving tomorrow. I pick out plump potatoes and veg and buy a packet of gravy. A pint of milk and a loaf of bread. Margarine. We leave with two heavy bags.

I can tell that Mark is anxious so I suggest we sit down for a coffee. It's not a real café – the village is too small for that – but there's a pub. There are benches outside on the pavement and a chalkboard with the promise of hot drinks. We sit down, bags between our knees, the shade keeping the groceries cool.

Our coffees arrive, complete with plastic-wrapped biscuits. I take mine out and dip it in the coffee, which is black and bitter and so hot that I burn my tongue.

We sit for a while making small conversation. "It feels like a proper village," I hear myself say. "I'm glad it's not one of those chocolate-box places. I'd hate to live in a museum."

This is all part of the plan, I tell myself.

"I like the pub," Mark says vaguely. His words bring with them a swell of potential. Us sitting by the fire with a hearty meal. Our distant neighbours at the bar with their dogs, which we'll have already met on walks in the woods. We'll come here together in winter, on a chilly weekend when it's too cold to work the garden outside. Muddy wellies. Feet stamping against the ice.

The sun is gentle on my skin. I close my eyes and try to pinpoint the exact spot where it stops being warm. I can feel the hairs on my arms, lying flat and smooth. But underneath, my muscles tighten, and I shiver despite myself.

Then unexpectedly, I say, "It was a Larsen trap."

Funny, how these words escape me before I remember why. And then I can see it: the dingy hunting shop on the corner of Edinburgh's Haymarket where my dad bought his fishing tackle. They had cages in there, hanging above the tills like herbs and bones hanging at an apothecary's. I remember the air that clung to those cages: masculine, hostile. The jovial banter of the shopkeeper always seemed to be at my expense. And the merchandise was so sinister, it felt taboo. Traps that would kill a rabbit in an instant. Camouflage overalls, the same ones that the army use. Pocket knives disguised as a carabiner or a belt. A lot of things in there you'd think were illegal, but they weren't. It's our human right to be permitted a small piece of destruction.

The coffee is nearing its end. There are dregs where I've dunked the biscuit, mixed with the cloudy stain of cheap grind. I push the cup away from me. Mark finished his some time ago. I think he's ready to leave.

"Can you take one of the bags for me?"

35

I ask it as a kindness, disguised as a request. I let him think he looks after me, the way I look after him.

We walk in a lopsided kind of way back to the woods. I wonder if anyone is watching us. Where do they think we're going, with our shopping bags, off into the middle of nowhere? Maybe they think we're travellers, camping out between the trees. Maybe they don't think anything at all.

We take a different path this time. I saw it marked on a map. A footpath, cutting through the older section of woodland.

The trees aren't uniform here and I'm glad. There's something easy about the way the branches grow together, matting like birds' nests where the brittle twigs catch. The effect is wild. *Natural*, I think to myself. Most of the trees are silver birch, but there's pine too, and the odd oak looking grand and stout as it sprawls out its leaves. The trunks are like ancient skin. Fingers rotting, like carrots forgotten at the back of the fridge.

The sun dips in and out of clouds. The sky is still blue and persistent through the gaps in the trees, but I'm filled with the feeling that it won't last long. Soon it will rain.

Mark walks next to me and I can feel the warmth coming off of him. There's a closeness here that feels foreign in the outdoor world. We walk as though we're lying in bed together, as though we're leaning against the kitchen countertops, mugs of tea in hand, sharing Sunday morning kisses. An arm, laced through mine. A palm clasping at the top of his sleeve. Our feet are so close that I think our knees might knock together, tripping ourselves up like tied shoelaces.

It's nice, this closeness. For a moment, it makes me forget. It was a good decision, to come here.

We've reached the end of the woodland path. We could trace it back into the trees and find another way home, or else it's back to the bridleway. We passed so many forks that we chose not to go down, opting for the thickest path that ran parallel to the track. Now the lines of trees stretch ahead of us, like rows of machinery. I swap the shopping bag to my other hand. I step onto the track.

The air is different on the main path to the old woods. It's a taste rather than sight or sound. It tastes like metal. Like iron rusting and breaking apart.

"Do you want me to take that?" Mark asks, nodding towards the bag.

"No, no. I'm fine."

"But I feel like you've got all the heavy stuff in yours."

"Don't be silly. The milk's in yours."

I bend my back, hoping that he won't notice. He'll think it's from the weight of the shopping, but it's not. It's just from the drive yesterday. My feet ache slightly inside of my boots. I'm not used to all this walking. But it's a good thing, I tell myself. We'll both be stronger, living here.

We pass the sections of the treelines. The woods are broken like blocks in a city grid. Then ahead, I can see the arm stretching off to the farmland where we found the crow. I know it's the same arm because it had a shrub of gorse at the end of it, breaching the uniformity. The thorns are dense, like rings of barbed wire. We're getting closer to the arm. I had hoped the forest path would allow us to avoid it. My heart is growing quicker. This isn't part of the plan.

Then it's right beside us. I can see without my eyes lifting: the dust picking up from the sandy grime; the cowslip and nettles that choke the space before the trees. *I won't look down it*, I tell myself. I'll keep my eyes on the ground and Mark will forget. *The bird will be gone and we'll be home. We'll be safe.*

But then, without knowing it, I've looked. My eyes are drawn towards it unwillingly, as if some deep part of my conscious has latched itself onto that bird in the cage. It's not the cage I see, but a sign, newly hammered into the ground. Red.

"Private property," it reads, and I read it out loud too – a mutter under my breath. I let the bags slump to the floor.

They knew we were here.

I hear Mark's breathing quicken.

They knew we were here, he's saying, but in pants of air that are hard to understand. They're looking for us. *They're coming to find us.*

"It's okay," I say to him. I rub my hands against his arms. The friction is warm. A glance back over my shoulder shows me the track. The birdcage is gone. "They must put up signs like that all the time."

"They know we did it," he tells me through gasps. "We shouldn't have come here. We shouldn't have come..."

I shake my head. My throat feels dry. My hands are cold, but Mark's arms are warm where our skin touches. I focus on that until my vision is blanched by warmth.

"It's just a misunderstanding," I hear myself say. I've got to calm him down so that we can get away from here. I glance down the road again, imagining an angry farmer. A man with a gun.

Mark's legs are shaking. He might collapse soon. He's done it before – in the frozen foods aisle of a supermarket; waiting in line to buy a bus ticket for a day out. He's sat down on the floor and refused to move, as though taking cover from a bomb or a hurricane. Eventually it got so bad that he wouldn't leave the house, not even to go to the corner shop to buy a pint of milk.

Please, I say in my head. Please don't do this now.

I close my eyes and take a breath. Anxiety is contagious. So is calmness. I grip my arms on his shoulders and force him to look at me. There. We're staring at each other and all I can see is brown speckled irises, his pupils dilating like a tunnel giving way to light.

We're breathing together, soft and easy. Eventually, Mark nods. An acknowledgement that he's okay now. Most of the time we speak like this – in shrugs and gestures, words failing us. I nod back and say, "Let's go home."

Home. It's funny how easy it is to say that, though we've only been here a day.

The green creepers are dancing in the wind as we slip through the gate. Their leaves bend towards us, bowing. The sun dips in and out of cloud, casting shadows against the white brick of the house. I uncurl my fingers through the bag when we reach the kitchen table. I put the milk away, the rest of the plastic carriers sitting conspicuous, like scraps of alien metal evidencing our invasion.

Mark hovers, trying to help. I tell him to sit down. It's easier for me to just get on with it. But now he's pacing, and I know that he'll only get worse if he tries to be still. I give him jobs. I make him feel useful. I want him to be happy in our new home.

I decide that I'll make shepherd's pie for tea. A nice, homecooked meal. We didn't buy any meat so it will have to be vegetarian. I tell Mark to get to work peeling the carrots while I put on the Aga. I stick my head in the burner and begin to feed it with gas.

"We should unpack the rest of the boxes," I tell him. My voice bounces off the metal, resounding around me, like I'm speaking into a tin can. *Job done.* Wiping my palms on my jeans, I stand up. Turn to face him. Mark is scratching his arm.

"And we'll need to set up the WiFi properly. The agency said an engineer would be out this afternoon. God knows what the last tenants did to break it... I'm going to Skype home tomorrow.

Just a test call, to check that everything runs smoothly."

His skin is red and blotchy. The blood fights against the surface. It raises itself in bumps.

"Stop it," I say. "You'll only make it worse."

Mark stops. He holds his hand taut. I see the white swell in his fingers – bony knuckles and gaunt bleached flesh.

I turn back to the Aga, to the pot that I've filled with water, the potatoes lined up to be peeled.

In the corner of my eye, I see him scratch.

We eat dinner at the table, pinned between cardboard boxes containing items of miscellaneous use. Our conversation is stilted, as it often is when I'm tired. To keep our spirits high, I write two lists on scraps of paper: one of tasks yet to be completed, and another of goals for our new future in the house.

On the first I write, *Organise bookshelf, Fix leak in shower pipe, Order shoe rack (price?), Unpack boxes, String washing line, Check satellite is working.*

On the second I write, *Walk to the moorlands, Walk to the old train tracks, Picnic on the hillside, Swim in the lochan, Plant vegetable patch, Plant flower garden, Repaint windows and latches, Bake bread in Aga, Forage fruits in forest.*

I lean back in my chair, looking at the list. Already I feel better.

41

Tonight I can't sleep. I'm thinking about the crow in its Larsen trap. In my mind's eye, I can't see it all at once. Only glimpses. I see the skin that's scraped off on its yellow legs, and the rings of red underneath. The wing where it's bent, catching in the steel bars, the feathers misshapen. The bead-like eyes, following me. I think of the word *clipped*.

Rain trums against the window. That's the only way I can describe it. It's not heavy enough to be called a drum, but *patter* is too light. It trums, making that sound. *Trr trr trr* against the glass.

I roll over.

Mark is sleeping facing me. His face so peaceful when he's like this that it's hard to think he's the same person. I picture him opening his eyes and pulling his arms around me. I picture his whites turning black like beads – like the eyes of the crow – piercing me through the dark.

I roll over.

The rose on the bush is hitting the window, too. I think that's what's keeping me up. Not the rain. Its pink petals haven't opened fully. It's the kind of rose you'd find alone in a vase. Clenched between lover's teeth. Spiny with thorns.

I wonder how long the roses last up here. I wonder if the noise will soften, once it's opened in full bloom. The wind must be cutting straight through the headland. That's why the rose is trumming. There's no shelter east of the house.

I think of thorns snagging at skin. Tiny wells of red, gathering at a pinprick. Thorns and scorns and mourns and adorns.

I wish I could switch off my brain.

II
PREMONITIONS

The rain has cleared by morning and the skies are washed a deep, clear blue.

The shopping arrives before midday. We set it out in rows on the table: which things need to go where. Mark takes the meat to the freezer, which is outside in the shed. I struggle to connect my laptop to the router.

Lights buzz and blink. The computer whirrs in complaint. It does not want to cooperate with this cottage, these old stone walls, this ancient plot of land. *We are here now,* I tell it. *You'll just have to work.*

Eventually, it gives in, and five little bars of signal appear in the corner of my screen.

I connect.

The video comes to life in a digital mirror. I see the cupboard doors behind me: mugs hanging from hooks; rows of spices and Mason jars. A blur on the lens distorts them. The camera flashes red, pinning my eye.

When the dial-tone rings, I jump in my seat. The motion makes Mark jump too, as he leans down to fetch another bag of groceries. His spine is taut for a second – then it relaxes. I accept the call.

Mum and Dad appear in front of me. They frown, holding the iPad clumsily, fingers obscuring half of the screen.

"Rosie? Rosie, can you see us?"

"I can see you."

"Put it down, stop that... Rosie? Ah, there she is." Dad, taking over. "How's the house, then? Did your shopping arrive?"

"Yes, it came just now. Mark's putting it away."

"Don't let him do all the hard work, Rosie," he says – for Mark's benefit, I'm sure.

"Are you settling in okay?" Mum asks.

"Fine, it's all fine. *Lovely*, actually. You would really like it here. Maybe once we're a little more settled, you could visit?"

"Oh, that sounds nice. Wouldn't that be nice, John?" She nudges Dad's arm.

"Very nice," he says gruffly.

Last bag, Mark mouths at me from the doorway.

"Nice weather we're having," Mum is saying. "I hope it keeps like this until the weekend."

"So much for April showers." That's Dad.

"How are things at home?" I ask the screen, readjusting my posture, one leg crossed beneath me. "Was your drive back alright?"

"Fine," Dad says. "Just fine."

"Yeah? Mum, how's Cassie doing?"

"She's—"

The image freezes, a blur of flesh. Mum has leant forwards, her face elongated, eyes stretched in a stream of pale grey. The pixels squirm and dance. Static air. I stare at her teeth – long, pointed, wolfish – as the white noise begins to screech.

SSSSSCC SCC SCA A SCC –

Jumping, jolting. Like pins pierced through metal. Needles into skin. Sharp, then gone.

Sharp, then gone. The image struggles to recalibrate. Teeth become longer, more pointed. Eyes blur into skin. In the same instant, the sun in the room vanishes. A cloud is passing overhead. The air feels cold now, the warmth sucked away. There's a pricking at the nape of my neck, creeping down my spine. I pull my jumper tight around me.

The video jumps back into place.

"... saying that we should really get her some company. But it's hard, we don't have the *space* for another dog. And Lord knows we don't have the energy for a puppy anymore."

The adrenaline spike begins to fall. Mum is human again, blotchy-faced, chattering happily about our old black lab. All is as it should be.

Focus on your breath.

Mark is at the door again, shutting it behind him, crossing the kitchen. He takes the orange juice from the fridge. I'm glad he didn't see the static. It would only set off his nerves.

Mum prattles on for half an hour before she lets me escape. I'm tired – tired from the rose on the window, tired from the downpour of rain. *Did it rain in the night?* Mark said this morning, kicking the mud from his boots, filling the kettle with water. Eyes heavy, mouth dry. I stared at him for a while before I heard the words.

Yes, I said. *It rained.*

One by one, we strike through the list. Boxes are unpacked and dismantled. Books are lined neatly on the shelves. Now we're working the garden, turning over plots of soil, digging beds for bulbs to lie. Mark has strung a washing line from the white-painted stone all the way to the elm tree. In absence of laundered clothes, I've hung a damp tea-towel to dry.

The sun is harsh today. It's unforgiving. I use my hand as a shield against it, squinting to the tiles of our roof. A bird has built a nest there. We'll have to clear the chimney if we want to light a fire.

There are beads of sweat on my forehead. Digging is hard work. Despite the sun and sweat, the day is cold. Our garden is unprotected from winds like this, which come in with force, relentless, cutting. The vines bow down to its might.

Mark follows my gaze. "What are you looking at?" he asks, eyes narrow and watery against the light.

"The roses," I say, because they've caught my attention now. "We need to cut them down."

Mark lets go of his spade. It wobbles slightly, but stays upright, rooted in a mound of earth.

"The roses? But they look so nice."

"They knock against the window at night. When it's windy. I can't get to sleep." I look at him, and his blank face is unbelievable. "Really?" I ask. "You haven't heard it?"

"No. When was this? Last night?"

Every night, I think.

He takes my silence as a yes.

"It probably just needs pruning," Mark says, but he sounds unsure of himself. We continue to stare up at the plant. "Don't cut it down completely. The landlord might want it kept up."

"No. Just around the window... Can you find me a ladder? I saw one somewhere. Maybe by the shed."

He obeys in silence. I blink and a solar flare catches my lashes, throwing a rainbow across the cottage wall. It will be a shame to get rid of the roses. For all the plants' waxy green foliage, there are only three flowers in bloom. They stand stark against the dead branches. Their petals are such a delicate pink. Mark returns with an extension ladder; the kind that we can prop up against the eaves.

"Careful of the crocus bulbs," I tell him as he fixes the base on steady ground. He gives me a wary look as I approach him, as though afraid that I'll ask him to climb up. There's a pair of shears in his hands. I reach for them, then reach for the ladder.

I extend it out to double its length, the top rungs swaying like tree branches. I hold it above me. It feels heavier now, up in the air, the weight of gravity accentuating it. The metal catches the wind, resisting like the sails of a ship. Mark holds out a hesitant hand to steady me, but I swipe him away. I need to focus.

The prongs catch the top of the roof. They dig into the gutter like teeth. I pull the rest of the ladder back, slightly slanted. I stamp its feet into the ground.

"Do you want me to hold it steady?" Mark says.

"Yes, okay."

Mark holds the base as I begin to climb. The ladder sits at an angle, a steady incline. Our house is not tall. This should make me feel better, but it doesn't. I'm too far away from the building. If I stretch out, I can barely reach the brickwork. The shears throw me off balance. I climb higher, higher, until I'm level with our bedroom window.

I can touch the bricks now. I put one palm against them, daringly, feeling the waxy paint above the rough stone. The rosebush is thick here. It's full of dead thorns: grey, parched branches of bramble that curl into one another. The leaves are laurel crisps, like paper withered by a flame, waiting for summer to revive them. And there, beside the drainpipe, I see the culprit of my sleepless night. I loop my arm through one of the rungs to open the clippers. Around the neck of the bud. I lean forwards, imagining that clean cutting sound. But instead there's a creak – a croak – a groaning of metal. The shears will not close.

I peer at them, looping an arm through the rungs of ladder for support. The blade is covered in rust; a plague of orange warts.

I open the shears to try again, leaning my weight against the ladder. My arms stretch through the rungs, and I peer through the gap at the rosebush. *Too low*, I think, climbing another step. I'm at the top of the window now, reaching over the rose. I press myself against the frame, knuckles knocking into brick as I pry the bud between the blades.

A wind whips past the cottage. It came out of nowhere, pushing clouds against the sun. The crawler shivers against it. The bramble shakes.

"Rosie?"

Mark's voice – from below me. I glance down and my vision swims. I am not high up, not really, but the distance is dizzying all the same.

I press the shears together, forcing the plates of iron to meet. The blades scrape. The metal groans. My head feels hot and cold both at once: the sun is hot, the wind is cold. The window is dark in front of me. Then, suddenly, rising from the darkness is a face.

A face.

It grins at me, feverish and maniacal. It is both there and not. It's the face of a girl, sitting on the bed, staring out towards me. Her eyes reach out to me, sparkling, maddening. With a start, I lean backwards. I'm caught off balance. My ankle slips.

The ladder slides from under my foot. I grasp out to the rosebush, gripping the necks of thorn. Below me, the ladder clatters. I hear Mark, panicking, hyperventilating. He screams out to me but I cannot see him. The rose-thorns cut into my hands. They scratch and scrape, tearing my palms, my wrists. The vine is not strong enough to hold me. My grip is slipping. My knees knock against the wall.

"Rosie!" he's shouting. "Rosie! Rosie! Rosie!" like the beat of a heart – the drum of the flower. He caws like a bird. He shouts other things too, but I can't hear them. The ground below is concrete. My knees will buckle if I drop. I need

Mark to move out of the way. I need to let go of the vine.

Red. The pain in my palms is sharp. The thud of my legs is dull. I close my eyes and I see the face in the window. Eyes shining, daggered; flesh and hair are blackened against the room. I let go of the branch and *drop.*

The ground finds me suddenly. It's closer than I thought – a mere second between mid-air and it. I land on my feet, knees bent, hands bleeding. I hold my palms up to me and pick the thorns out. I'll have blisters for days.

Mark is shaking all over. *Are you alright?* He's saying. *Are you okay?*

I straighten up so that my spine is tall. The ladder is unbroken on the slabs of stone. Mark is hugging himself, arms clutched around his stomach, telling me that it's his fault.

I stare up to the wall above – to the vacant window where there is nothing but black. The rose still hangs there, shaking in the wind.

I cannot tell Mark about the face. It will only worry him. There is no need to make him fret. We are safe here. Nothing can hurt us now.

I stare at my reflection in the bathroom mirror. Look – my eyes are wet with tears. I think of them sharpened, hollowed, fresh with pain. I think how the rest of my face would be swallowed by the dark of the room. Yes, I think to myself. It was only me; it was just a reflection. We are alone here, and nothing can hurt us now.

They hang rabbit's feet above the doors in the village. It's a good omen, meant to ward off evil spirits. Two little bunny toes pinned to the oak wood like the palms of Christ. My hands are battered and scratched from the rose bush. I wipe them on my trousers as we duck inside. Pain pinches as I stretch my skin against the fibres of my jeans.

Mark didn't want to go to the pub today. He was in one of his dark moods, lying on his side, refusing to get out of bed. He stared at the wall in front of him: the creamy white plaster, misshapen the way that old houses can be. The light from the window teemed in on him, casting a halo on the back of his head. Up, I said. You'll feel better if we're out.

We walked through the forest the long way, keeping careful track of the winding paths. The sun is still bright and shining. I begin work tomorrow. I'm determined to make the most of this last day.

When we get to the pub, we find a bench at the back of the bar. I order us a pint of beer each. When they arrive, Mark shakes his head.

"One won't hurt," I tell him.

"My tablets," he says.

His eyes are cast down at the table. I shrug and take his pint from him, placing it next to my own. Two men at the bar nudge each other and turn to us. They're whispering something. *Look at the newcomers,* I imagine they say. *How long will they last?*

And maybe other things too. Things about Mark. About his condition. I need to protect him from this. It's my job to shield him.

"Don't listen to them," I say.

He looks up, quizzical. Then he throws a look over his shoulder to the two men, who promptly glance back to their beers.

"What were they saying?" Mark asks me.

"Nothing," I lie.

"No, what was it?"

"You don't want to know."

I take a glug of my beer, annoyed. Today was going to be so perfect. I had it all planned out: our lazy walk, our leisurely lunch in town. I want to spit at the men by the bar. I want to throw the pail of lager at them, to see them drenched in beer.

"What's wrong?"

"Nothing."

"You're agitated," Mark says. There is something so witless in his voice, so oblivious. How can he only just be realising this? How can he be so willingly blind?

I scrunch my nose up as I sip the beer. It's not Mark's fault. I know this. I remind myself every day. I let the words wheel round and round until they *click*. But sometimes it feels as though he could at least *try*.

"Are you angry with me?" Timid – shameful.

"Of course I'm not angry."

"You're angry. I can tell."

I give him a look that's more like a snarl. Teeth bared, like an animal. I see the way he shrinks backwards, the way he retreats inside of himself, like a tortoise into its shell.

I'm ruining it. I'm ruining this perfect life we've made.

Another sip. I let out a sigh.

"I'm not angry. Just tired."

"You didn't sleep again?" He's alert now: perceptive, empathic. He reaches forward for my hand and holds it in his, his calloused thumb making circles on the back of my hand.

"No."

"What's keeping you up?" he asks. His voice is soft, coaxing me back to him. It's easy to forget, after everything that's happened, the people we used to be.

I let myself talk.

"That stupid rose," I'm saying. "I don't know how you don't hear it. It's driving me mad."

He squares his shoulders, wincing slightly at my choice of words. His thumb pauses for a moment, then continues its circle in reverse.

"Maybe we could open the window? Cut it from inside?"

"You can try," I say wearily. "I couldn't reach it earlier."

"Or I could go up the ladder?"

It's a noble suggestion, but I purse my lips together. Shake my head. I can't let him do that.

Mark turns my hand over and pries open my fingers. The scratches are thin, like scarlet wires. He bends down and kisses my palm, then leans back.

"What do you want to do this afternoon?" he asks.

He is trying to make me feel better. Trying to play his part. I love him so much for it. Sometimes it feels like I can't contain all my love. But at the same time, it makes me sad: sad that he is obligated to feed me this line, sad that I know it's just a game. The perfect day is already lost. It's better to let it slip away.

"We don't have to do anything."

"We could go to the lochan, if you want? The swimming lake. If we head straight there we'll be back before it's dark."

"No, no. Let's do that next weekend. So that we can enjoy it properly."

"A film then? The TV is set up now. We can watch whatever you want."

I stare at the brickwork on the wall: the old slabs half-concealed with paint and plaster. I feel the beer churning in my stomach; an empty fizz, wearing thin. "I don't mind."

Mark continues to talk to me until our food arrives. He asks questions, knowing my answers have little consequence, anything to keep the silence at bay. When we finally leave the pub, and the village, he leads me through the trees back home.

"Look," he says, pointing to the lichen on the trees. "The air quality must be good here."

Look: wild strawberries. The first of the season.

Look: a thrush has made her nest here.

Look.

Look.

Look.

When we reach the cottage, the mirage slips. The rose bush is thick and grey, full of dead branches. The wall is chipped, smoke-stained, ugly. Our boots will drag mud into the cottage and trail it through the passageways. It's stamped into the carpets.

"I'll put on a film," Mark says. "And blankets. That'll be nice, won't it?"

I don't want the blankets brought downstairs. The fabric isn't right. The polyester will pick up our sweat, hold it hostage in its fibres. It doesn't go with the sofas, which are cotton grey, minimal, bare. I think this but I don't say it.

TV on. Chatter of noise. Why are we afraid of silence?

Mark makes dinner. He stands in the kitchen, hand scratching the back of his neck, wincing at the shelves of food. "What do you want to eat?"

A memory from Before. I see Mark (only he's not Mark) standing by the oven. Pan in hand. Cherry tomatoes; garlic; salt. Wide grin – that's gone now. Hair long (now it's short). My arms wrap around him, breathing him in. Mark, only he's not Mark, smiles.

"I don't mind," I say.

Soup, then. Tin cans poured into bowls. Three minutes microwaved. Chunks of vegetables, floating in brine. *Serve hot, with bread.*

I think of the pie I planned to make. The meat, still in the freezer. The pastry, ready rolled, turning sour in the fridge.

The plan is slipping out of reach.

And the TV drones endlessly on, the talk-show host laughing at a joke I don't understand.

Mark squeezes my thigh and smiles at me. I can see it, my thigh below me, thick white roll of flesh, pulled tight as it curves towards my groin. I can see his hands, squeezing, pushing aside the itchy trim of the throw. The way his elbow bends into the crevice of sofa. The hairs of his arm, bowed, like reeds in a tide. Below: the worn cotton, the scratch of carpet, the hard wood of the floors. Then up, his eyes, his round, soft lips. Tugging at the corners. Skin pinched straight.

I also see two figures on a sofa. A man, trapped in an underwater world, trying to surface, trying to smile. A woman, seeing nothing at all.

The next day is better. Funny how the storm clouds can gather, dense, impenetrable, then suddenly disperse.

I drink coffee in the garden, though it is frigidly cold, listening to the chattering of the birds. There are dozens of them, *swarms* of them, black bodies hunched over in the trees, squawking and prattling as they build their nests. I don't think I've ever seen so many birds.

They're crows, I think. Or are they rooks? Rooks are bigger – yes, I can see the difference now. There are both crows and rooks, roosting in the elm tree. The tree's bark is patchy and coarse. The dregs of coffee are like grains of soil on my tongue.

Work. I dreaded it so much and now it's here. The end of our blissful interlude. A honeymoon, stoppered shut.

I turn inside as the rooks rise from their perches. Their caws carry across the skies. I lock the latch. Turn on the laptop. The pixels come to life. The fan begins to whirl. Login and password, if you please.

"Morning," says Mark as my emails load. He rubs his eyes, sleepily, retrieving the milk from the fridge door.

"Morning."

Dear Rosie,

I'm meeting with a client at 12 noon today and thought you might like to join us over the phone.

"Did you get bread in the end?"

"In the tin below the china rack."

Attached is a draft report for Thursday's submittal. Please could you look this over and let me know any changes ASAP.

Mark fumbling – a clattering of pans.

Dear Rosie,

"Did you sleep well?"

Boil of the kettle. The toaster pops.

"Fine."

I tap my fingers against the keyboard, writing a hasty reply.

"You?"

Mark's saying something, but I don't hear it. My eyes jump across the screen to another email, separating business from junk.

The chair *scrapes*. And butter, scratching the surface of bread. So many emails – don't they know I've just moved house? Already it feels like a mistake. I've had too long off. I've fallen behind.

Dear "Rosie? Are you listening?"

Head in hands. I grasp at my hair, pulling it taut. Like tufts of grass from a garden. Pulling daisies. I look up at Mark.

"What?"

He looks swiftly down.

"You're mad at me."

"No I'm not."

"You are. I'm sorry. You're trying to work."

"No," I say, pushing the laptop away. The screen dances in my periphery. *Do you want to save as draft?*

"I'm sorry, I–"

His voice is rising, his breath shallow, turning to gasps. I put my hand over his firmly: enough pressure to stop him short. I look at him, into his blue-grey eyes. Flecks swim in them. Head above water. Keep breathing, I think to him.

Today will be better.

"It's alright," I say, and I keep my voice smooth. I inhale then exhale; my palm still clasped over him. I shut my eyes, smiling, guiding him. *There, like that.* We're breathing in time now. "It's alright. I'm here."

Mark opens his eyes after I do. He blinks, pupils dilating, flickering around the room. He looks like a child searching for something; like an old man who has lost his train of thought.

I keep my voice soft as honey. Any change in decibel, in inflection or tone, and the mirage will shatter. "I just have to do some work for a bit, but I'll be here if you need me."

He nods, accepting. His toast has turned cold. I glance at it, and he does too, and his hand moves from underneath mine. I feel the skin where we touched moisten then cool. He's eating his toast now, staring at it with quiet fascination, his chews deliberate and slow. How wrapped up in his own mind he is, in his own orbit, his own gravity, when moments ago we were aligned. How quickly I too, pulling my laptop towards me, cross into another world.

There is so much to do.

Archives need sorting, storing and tagging, placed into folders for scholars to find. There are emails to reply to: meetings to virtually attend, or otherwise send apologies. Applications from new readers to approve. A journalist, requesting access to a newspaper backlog that we do not store; a council-worker who has clearly mistaken me for somebody else.

Hasty replies. PDF copies, dragged and dropped. My computer buzzes on the table, self-sufficient, whirring as it works. I walk to the sink for a glass of water. To the bedroom for a jumper – the bathroom to use the loo. I don't know where Mark has gone. I picture him out in the garden, raking the flower beds, wiping sweat from his brow. The image brings with it a swell of envy.

The kitchen is dark; cramped. The squat windows don't let in enough light. Then, when they do, the effect is blinding. When I join a video call, I'm bleached white with sunlight, swallowed by it, drowning in it. Then all of a sudden the screen calibrates and I'm nothing more than a blocked silhouette.

I work through lunch, eating a sandwich as I watch the files upload. One meeting, then another. Then I'm done.

I sit at the kitchen table, staring at the case of my laptop, silver edge chipped where I dropped it last year. I've done it. A day of work. I realise now how worried I've been. Worried that the two worlds can't be forced together: that they'll hold their own like magnets, or drops of stubborn oil in a boiling pot. But I have done it. We are here.

The evening slips by like liquid. The sun sets, the sky bathed pink then deepening in blue. Mark jabbers on about his day and I listen, content, mug of camomile tea in hand. I think of the flowers I'll plant in the garden, and what we'll do at the weekend. The lochan, we decide.

Then, before I know it, it's night – the darkness; the rose bud – and then it's morning again.

Coffee, toast, laptop. Mark is coming downstairs as I log onto the portal. He stretches, eyes thick with sleep. I skim the application I'm to sign, mind skipping over phrases. Mark takes his tea outside.

Work – rest – the rose on the window.

The emails come in flurries: midmorning, before the first coffee break; then hastily at ten to five. As the days tick by, I feel myself grow restless. The house feels too small, the ceiling too low. The walls are too close together. I long to be outside again. At lunch, I take walks along the edge of the woods. Between meetings, while the files drag and drop, drag and drop, I stand on the patio below the rose bush. There's a scratch on the paving stones where the ladder smacked down. I lace my hands through the scrawny leaves. The cracks between the concrete are crowded with nettle-green leaves. I think of what they'll look like in the months to come: small flecks of lilac; creeping charlie and chickweed and empty arms of pennycress. By the wall, there'll be wild daisies and dog violets. At the moment, the colours are sparse, but over the next weeks and months they will brighten, they will thicken, they will bloom. The trees are still mostly skeletal. The canopies are regaining their green, sprouts of leaf emerging from bone. In the woods, you can already feel it: the birdsong lifting up into the trees, the subtle sway of branches. The air feels lighter in the forest. Here, it's sharp. Cutting. The sun is bright and fierce and cold. But summer will come.

Dog violets, I tell myself. And columbine and harebells and thistles, cornflower blue. Honeysuckle climbing the doorframe. Tufts of yarrow in the cracks of the wall.

Then the vision passes. Back to work.

"How is it going?" Mark asks on Thursday. We're sitting in the living room, the TV on for background noise, plates of spaghetti on our laps.

"Good," I tell him. "Better than I expected."

"Oh yeah?"

"Yeah."

"You're not sorry I made us leave?"

He tries to say it casually, but I can hear the strain in his tenor — the way his voice wavers, a pitch higher than usual, threatening to break.

"Not at all. If anything, it makes me wonder why we didn't do this sooner."

He grimaces. My reassurance is *too* much, *too* kind, he needs to push it away.

We slurp at our spaghetti. A streak of orange stains Mark's chin.

"It's all going to work out then?" he asks after a beat.

"Yes," I tell him. "I think that it will."

Friday comes. Glorious Friday; a Sabbath. The tightrope I walk between two worlds is loosening, becoming slack, giving way. I can almost feel the ground beneath me. *Grounded.* I grind my teeth together. Focus on the last of my tasks.

Mark hovers around me all day. He's agitated, I know. I can feel it in the way the air moves around him. It's soft, soft, soft, then *brittle.* Thorny and corrosive, like hairs standing on end.

It was like this in our old place. Him, always wanting something. Never knowing how to ask for it. Maybe not knowing what it was at all that he needed from me. And me, trying to work, trying to think, trying to breathe. I send off an email and scrape back my chair.

It's not just library work that needs doing. There are clothes to launder, dishes to wash, sheets that need hanging up to air and dry. We've been here over a week now and it's beginning to show. A pair of trousers, thrown lazily over the banister rail. An odd sock kicked under the sofa. Jumpers and jackets piling on the backs of chairs.

It goes without saying that Mark can do none of this. He cannot dust and clean and sweep. He cannot kneel down at the base of the shower and pick hairs from the drain. Of course I would not ask him to. He is too fragile, too delicate, for any of this. But he hovers all the same, like a hornet, like a moth, asking how he can ease the burden. "Let me help you with that," he says, as I push past with a pile of laundry. "Tell me what I can do," as I slam shut the dishwasher door.

But I don't mind these tasks. They keep me busy, while I wait for a file to upload, for the pasta to cook, for the router to reconnect. They keep me sane, I tell myself, and that's the greatest reward of all.

On Saturday a storm breaks. We won't go swimming after all.

I sit inside, watching the rain trickle down the windows. The gutter gargles, overrun. Streams gather on the driveway, splitting the gravel into tributaries, like veins. Mark is sitting at the sill, head pressed against the glass. He has a book in his hands but I can tell he's struggling to read it. He turns the page back and forth, back and forth.

I can't help but feel cheated. All week I have sat here, hunched over the table, straining against the dim kitchen light. And now that I'm free, the heavens have opened.

The universe has a bigger plan, I tell myself as the raindrops run into each other, dividing and multiplying in a secret code. I study the waterdrops as though they are a map. A sign from above. A message encrypted for me alone. *You are a raindrop in an ocean. You are part of the Master Plan.*

A day at home, then. There is no point mourning what could have been – that abstract future which never truly existed, but still looms like a shadow in my mind. Cast it out. *Begone.* I close my eyes, thinking of how lush the grass will be after this downpour. How the air will be fresh and clean. We'll open the windows and doors, I think.

And what to do until then? What to do...

Aha! A lightbulb moment, like a crack of lightning blazing against a storm. I remember. When we unpacked, I found an old cardboard box in the wardrobe upstairs, covered in a skin of dust. A board-game left over from whoever lived here before. And cocoa, in the larder, which I can heat over the stove. I jump up, making Mark start. No time to apologise – I'm already up the stairs!

I find it exactly where I first saw it, only now it's tucked behind the leather suitcase and our walking shoes. I lift it carefully, minding the spare coat-hanger that's fallen down, and hold it in front of me, under the grey, rainy light. With one hand, I wipe the dust away.

The box is faded pink, like a salmon beginning to turn bad. It might have been scarlet once, or burgundy, or maroon. But time has bleached the box pink. There's a water-spot in one corner where damp has warped the title.

Downstairs.

Mark has left the windowsill. He's standing in the living room, unsure of what to do, of his place in my plan. The ceiling is half an inch too low for him. He has to hunch his shoulders over so as not to be hit by the light.

"What's that?" he asks, seeing the board in my hands.

"A game I found. I thought we could play."

I sit cross-legged on the carpet and begin to unpack the box. The board itself is folded twice. At full-size, it covers nearly the width of the rug.

Mark sits beside me. He picks up one of the counters: an old man with a stick. "What are the rules?"

"I don't know yet. Let's check we have all the pieces first."

I count each piece. There are thirteen: exactly as there should be. The board shows a forest path, winding through mountains and ravines. In one corner is a cottage. At the opposite is a town. There's a clock-face in the middle with eyes and a mouth. It's sinister in a childish way: the eyes are too knowing. The smile is too thin.

There's an instruction manual which I read aloud, though parts of the ink are bleached out from water. There's a deck of chance cards, also. Mark picks one from the pile, revealing the carcass of an animal, ribs cracked open and exposed. "What kind of game is this?" he says.

"A children's game. Apparently. Shall we do a practice round, first? To check we know the rules?"

The rules – it turns out – are actually quite simple. There's a plastic dial that should spin on the clock's face, but that part is lost, so we decide to play without it. The day slips by like water. We have one game, then two, and then I decide to make the cocoa. Lunch at the table. Dishes cleaned and dried. Washing to be hung, in the absence of sunshine, on every crag we can find: every door, every handle, every chair, is subject to a jumper, a t-shirt, a towel. The chandelier in the living room, made of iron and fitted with a single electric bulb, becomes a rack for boxer shorts and tights and socks. Its metal curls are like meat hooks. Wet washing drips like blood. By the time we eventually sit down again to play our third round of the game, it's almost dark.

"Funny," I say to Mark as we set up the board. "It feels like the day had only just started."

"Time flies," he says, letting the rest of the idiom evaporate. He moves the pieces expertly into their places on the board. He won the last two games. "You start, this time."

I roll the dice. Six steps forward.

"That means you get another go."

Six.

Six.

He hovers over me as I move my counter: a young girl in a nightdress, flowers in her hair. Is she a witch of some kind? An enchantress? I picture her, drifting like a ghost through the woodland. She collects feathers beneath the branches. Her pockets are filled with bones.

"Pick a card."

"Alright," I snap. "I know."

I pick the card up and turn it over. We're both allowed to see, but I want to peak at it first.

I see first the pale blue sky. The cream white wings and the black, hollow eyes. A sprout of leaf between its pincered beak. A splash of colour: red and yellow and green and blue. *Sunshine after rain.*

I move through the forest.

Mark rolls three.

Pick a card, any card. Though I can't see it this time. He holds it close to his chest.

My turn. But I roll the wrong number. I can't move.

Through the woods, our counters a dance. We turn over card after card, laying them out on the carpet. Faded eyes stare at us, blank. Like characters from a fairy tale: the Hermit, the Hanging Man. And Death, and Peace, and the Sun.

He's chasing my heels. He's nearly caught up. It's dark already. Outside, the thunder cracks. With a start, I think of the face I saw last week. Of the window upstairs, and the ladder slipping from my feet. Mark's hands slipping –

71

dropping – retreating in shock. A crash below. Burnt, ripping skin.

Why didn't he hold tighter?

"Rosie. Are you going to move your piece?"

The shadows are growing on the walls. The darkness gathers. I push the counter over – Mark's counter, the one closest to me. Its head hits the board with a *click*, just under the '5' of the clock.

"What was that for?"

"I don't feel like playing anymore."

I gather my cardigan around me, lifting myself up from the floor. My knees crack. Has the room always been this cold?

"Can't we finish the game?"

"No. I don't want to."

"I was having fun."

I stare at him. My eyes bore into his. I imagine what I look like. Wild, unruly. Like the vines that swallow the walls of the board-game cottage, or the shoots of gorse that line the forest floor like snakes.

It's only a second that I look at him like this. Only a second, because I see how it upsets him. And the last thing I want is for him to be upset.

"I'm just tired," I tell him, gaze dropping to the floor. To the hairs that cling to the rug. The scuffs where we brought mud in.

"Okay," says Mark.

"Can you help me clear this up?"

We pack the board away, folded twice, counters collected and stored in the grey-pink box. I can't find my playing piece. It must have been knocked off the cardboard when I pushed over Mark's piece. Mark is on his knees, searching for it under the sofa legs.

"Leave it," I say. "I want to go to bed."

The rain is thinning now, sprinkling down in a vapour. It hisses like steam. The wind has wrapped itself around the cottage. It moans, low and guttural. Then, piercing and shrill, it screams through the trees.

I turn off the lights, room by room. I check the bolt on the door. We left a window open in the bathroom upstairs, and the rain has poured in, fat splatters glistening black against the sill. I stick my head out to feel the air. It's a thick, dampened aether. I can feel the spittle of clouds as I waff my hand through it, catching the latch. Closed and locked.

Teeth brushed. Pills poured into hands. Mark fills up a cup with water. He gulps and swallows. He really needs to wash that mug. I can see the sticky line where his mouth presses against it.

And the pills, tightened and sealed, Mark putting them back in the cabinet where they belong.

I catch his arm.

"Can I have one?"

He blinks at me. "One of my tablets?"

"The sleeping pills. I've been waking up a lot since we moved."

His hand hovers there, on the lid. His knuckles are clutched around the plastic cap, taut, turning white. Then his arm turns slack.

"Sure. Just one though. They make you feel groggy if you take them too often."

"Thanks."

He shakes one into my hand, a single white pill. I swallow it dry. It scratches its way down my throat. Water? Mark asks, ready to fill his mug. I shake my head.

The wind continues to howl. The branches on the rose bush shake. I wait to be pulled into oblivion.

III
REVELATIONS

III

REVELATIONS

The lane has become a sea of mud. It is thick and squelchy. I nearly lose a shoe crossing onto the lane. The clouds hang low and ominous, pressing down on us, squashing the whole atmosphere to half its size. The rain has stopped, but the storm still gathers.

It's not the weather for walking. The forest paths are far too flooded. On the track, potholes become craters. Puddles stretch, wide as streams. Then, further down, where the road meets the bridge, the lane has been swallowed completely. I'll be drenched if I try to cross it. But I am also restless. I need to leave the house.

This is why I end up walking over the fields. I am on the phone again, more for comfort than anything else. Mum is nattering on about the neighbours, about her sewing club, about how I wouldn't *believe* the state the garden's become. Her voice crackles in and out as I trudge along the hedgerows. My boots will be ruined by the time I'm home.

I turn right past the farmland, then left, then right again, following the path of least resistance. A maze determined by whichever patch of ground looks most firm.

I can no longer see the cottage, but I see the trees that surround it: a pin on a map, marking home. There are no other buildings for miles and miles – unless you were to cut down the forest and march towards the village. There's just this: fields and hedgerows and the occasional tree. Then, behind me, the black line of the woods.

Branches, so thick that light won't penetrate, twisted together in knots, *black black black* and then not. The forest stops abruptly, as though unwilling to cross some invisible line entrenched in the soil.

What I mean is, the landscape is barren. That's why it's a surprise when I see the jeep parked in the corner of the field, and a man in a thick khaki raincoat walking towards me.

"Private land," he calls from several metres away. It's unnerving, the way he cuts straight to it. Like he's reading the title of an email before the main body of text.

"I'm sorry, I didn't know. We've just moved in..."

I'm moving towards him still, trying to explain. I gesture towards the huddle of trees where our cottage should be. Funny, you'd think you could see it from here. The trees should not be so tall or wide.

"I know who you are," the man says. His voice is gentler now that he's close. He lifts his cap and I realise that I know him too. It's our landlord: the man who owns the cottage. "That's still no excuse to be roaming around my fields."

"You're right, I —"

"No need to explain yourself. I just kindly ask that you leave." He puts his hat back on and tilts his head, playing the gentleman. Behind him, I see a dog prancing, trying to escape its chain. Next to the dog is a strange, metal object. Some kind of cage.

Rosie? Mum says on the other end of the line. *Rosie, are you still there?*

"Yes. Of course. It won't happen again."

His eyes are on me as I turn away. I can feel them, on my back, like a laser homing in on its target. X marks the spot.

"Still here, Mum," I say to the phone.

"Oh, good. I thought I might have lost you."

She carries on, oblivious to my encounter, happily self-centred as she relays the gossip of the town. I mumble agreement, confusion, surprise. But I find I can no longer focus on her words. I'm thinking about the landlord, about the dog and the cage. There is something sinister about it. Something that feels sour, like milk on the turn.

Water seeps into my boots. I'm taking the short way back, muddy as a bog. I can see the sycamore tree ahead; the one I'll picnic under when its dry again.

"Well?" Mum is asking. "What do you think I should do?"

"I'm sorry, Mum, I lost you for a second there. Tell it to me again?"

"I was just saying that Angie is having problems—"

SSSSSSSSCCCCCCCCHHHHHHH

Screeching – deafening – *dead*. Like something trying to break into my brain. I hold the phone away, wincing as my ear drum pulses. The white noise screams like static in my head. Then, just as suddenly as it came, it stops.

I turn the phone over. The screen is black. The battery must have failed. I clench the buttons tight, willing it to life. Nothing.

I stare up, to the canopy above me. There are rooks sitting in the high branches, chattering, unfurling their feathers. I stare at one, who is pecking at the leathery skin of its foot. It cocks its head, as though sensing it's being watched. Then, in one swift turn of its neck, it looks at me. Its insect eyes pierce into mine. The chattering stops.

I stamp my boots at the threshold. I kick them off and slam the door shut. My phone clicks into the charger. Nothing, nada, zero. The screen does not come to life.

"What's wrong?" Mark asks from the doorway.

"My stupid phone. The battery's flat and now the charger won't work."

"Here. Let me have a go."

I drop the charger, moving over. Mark takes his time staring from phone to cable – a two-piece puzzle that neither of us can solve.

"Did you drop it in water?"

"No."

"Are you sure?"

"Yes, I'm sure!"

"It looks like it might be water damaged. We could put it in rice?"

I want to say something sarcastic, but I bite my tongue back. Resist the urge. *He's only trying to be helpful. And maybe it will work.*

"Fine. I'll get the rice."

The rice does not work. My phone is yet to come to life. We have tested both chargers – Mark's and mine. His phone responds to both, and my phone to neither. It is a flatline. A lost cause.

I spend most of Monday morning shopping for a new one, my emails open in a separate tab. Few companies deliver to a place like this free of charge. I wonder whether it's best waiting until we go to town proper. There's a bus that goes from the village to the station, and from there it's one stop on the train.

When will be the next chance? Two weeks? Three? It seems a shame to leave the cottage so soon – this slice of Eden that we've carved for ourselves. But needs must.

Can I survive that long without a phone? I suppose I'll have to. It might be good for me, going offline. Off the grid – into the wild. Isn't that what I want?

A blessing, then, in disguise.

The rain started up again sometime in the night. It started long after moon rising, when the shadows filled the room like ink in a pot. Sleep came to me in snatches. And then there was light – fierce, grey, sodden with rain.

"Are you busy?" Mark asks as I load up the archives. My phone sits between us, laid to rest on its bed of rice.

"I have a meeting in 15."

"Okay."

He stands behind me, biting his lip. I can see his reflection in my monitor. I don't look up.

"What is it?"

Weight shifted from one foot to another. "What are you doing this evening?"

"I don't know." Shit. I've saved the document in the wrong folder. The internet strains as I attempt to move it. "Why?"

There's a film on BBC at 9. A murder mystery. Mark wonders if we want to watch it?

I resist the urge to sigh. "Is that all?"

"We don't have to," he says, suddenly anxious. His voice is rising in pitch. He begins to scratch his arm.

"Mark."

"I just thought I'd ask."

I turn to face him. "*Mark.*"

His eyes are wide and pitiful. I can't be mad at him when he's like this. I'm about to tell him that of course we can watch it – that I'm not mad at him – but that I wish he would just *think for himself* sometimes. But we're caught off guard. Outside, the wind is wailing. The glass rattles. The storm has the cottage snared, shaking it like a child rousing its mother from sleep. It demands our attention. Both Mark and I glance up.

A flicker of black in my periphery. The tree branches are bowing in the gale. Any buds of spring will be torn from their arms. It's a wonder the saplings haven't been torn from their roots.

"Do you want to check the windows upstairs are locked?"

Mark nods, eager to obey my command. I can hear him on the stairs when the thunder cracks.

It's a white spark – nothing like the low, grey rumbles of Saturday. Bright and white and immediate, like pressing your hand down on a hot stove. I blink and still I can see it: like stars, filling the corners of my eyes.

The house is silent for a second. There are no footfalls upstairs. My laptop stops humming. We are all holding our breath.

Then *release*.

The rain continues to drum against the windowpanes. I hear Mark, rushing, almost stumbling, banging shut shutters and clicking locks into place. The *ping* of an email. Another growl of thunder, this time from further away. Hissing wind. Shivering walls.

I open up Skype for my meeting. The loading screen is too bright, too synthetic, for this dim room. The messages pile in, scarlet red. Then a phone dial rings, disjointed, electric. *Incoming call.* I accept.

My line manager appears, disfigured in a series of pixels. His voice crackles: ice thawing, frosty branches *snapped*. The image tugs one way, then another, before settling like the fizz of soda effervescing, into place.

"Ah, Rosie. I can see you now. Can you hear me ok?"

"Yes. Sorry, the WiFi isn't great here."

"Not a problem. Now, did you want to catch me up on the LaVeyan archives?"

I talk him through my work from the past week: how I've categorised the records; which articles are yet to be processed online. The table rattles against the barricade of wind. It's hard to hear through the rain. I press my palms on the table, on my laptop, trying to hold it steady. In my periphery I see the door isn't bolted properly. One more gust and it could blow off its latch. *Where's Mark?*

Then the thunder – closer now – closer, closer. My manager is waiting for an answer. The screen jumps, then refocuses.

"I'm having trouble hearing you," I speak into the microphone. "Can you say that again?"

A white flash. Blinding – brilliant. A vision of angels. A glimpse of God. It blazes, burnt in my retinas, but it is cold and biting as ice.

Then a sudden darkening, darkening, as my eyes struggle to calibrate to the room surrounding them. The old, worn beige of oak and pine. The low, hollow ceilings, closing in, cave-like. The lights have gone out. And my computer screen, black. An electronic death.

My heart is hammering against my ears. I can feel its pulse, trembling, as though the lightning struck *me*. My hands shake too, turned into branches on the trees outside, turned into panes of glass, readying to *crack*. My finger finds the trackpad, attempting to jurr the screen back to life.

From above, footsteps. A throb, travelling across the ceiling, moving down the stairs. Mark appears in the doorway.

"Did the power just go out?"

"And the internet."

The mouse appears on my laptop screen – a single curser of light against a swarm of black. *System restart.*

"Do you want me to go check the fuse box?"

The fuse box; in the cellar. We haven't been down there yet.

"I'll go with you."

I find a box of matches and go upstairs to fetch a candle. *Strike* – bright white. The flame wafts the stale scent of vanilla. I cup my hands around the jar, rimmed ochre with smoke. The glass is hot against the flare.

The door to the basement is along from the stairs. The paint is chalk and chipped, like bone or teeth. Its hinges are beginning to rust. From below is the stench of hollowness: damp and dust-ridden, like a cave. We walk down the stairs – I in front, Mark my shadow. The howling wind becomes hush as we descend into the earth.

Underground. There will be worms the other side of these walls, and roots, and dead things. The candlelight flickers, trembling. The light is golden against my hands. The air is cold and hollow, like a crypt. There is solace in its silence.

The fuse box sits on the western wall. Water runs down the stone, which is bare of plaster. There are streaks of black and green. Whether these colours are real or distorted under the candlelight, I cannot tell. I pass the flame to Mark and ask him to hold it close. Then I flick the switches, one by one. Jumpstart.

"Should I check upstairs? See if it's worked?"

"We'll both go," I tell Mark. The flame has dampened. It's nearly extinguished. I don't want to be left alone in the dark.

Up the stairs and into the dim light. The windows rattle again, the storm persistent. Mark reaches for the light switch and flicks it down. Nothing happens.

He clicks it up again, then down once more. Up, down, up, down, up.

"Enough," I say, hand on his arm. "Let's try the fuse box again. Maybe I missed something."

We relight the candle with another match. Then back into the cellar; back into the dark. The second attempt is no more successful than the first. On the third performance of the ritual, striking a match and watching the shadows grow as the wick sizzles to life, I notice the thin slice of window in the corner of the room. There, through overgrown bracken and weeds, I can see the phantom shapes of the garden. A wooden telegraph pole dangles limp at the foot of the trees, a web of cables and wire tangled around the arms of its head.

"What is it?"

Mark, beside me, registers the pole. We can just about make out its body, swaying in the wind like a corpse, the knots that hold it asphyxiatingly tight.

"That might be a problem," he says.

It does not escape me, the quiet calm of his comment. The problem seems so large, so extraneous, that there is no use fretting about it. All we can do is wait for the storm to pass.

I give a quick nod. "A problem," I agree. "I think there are more matches upstairs."

An evening passes in candlelight. We are living in a séance, in a portal to a darker time.

The storm quietly raging is as unnoticeable as breath. When we slip into the sheets and blow out the last torch, it is like an exhale.

A day, waiting in the cottage. The board game set up on the living room carpet. The laptop, in fruitless attempts to connect to the internet, drains its battery to sixty-seven percent.

And then the night comes again, and the wind stops howling. The rain stops spitting at the windows. Even the rose is still.

I stand at the window, watching the crack in the curtains where the clouds wander across the sky. The turning of planets, the shimmering of stars. Then the misty vapours disperse completely, leaving only moonlight, soft, silver moonlight, drenching the room in silent water.

Light.

When I wake up, I've almost forgotten about the power cut. About the internet, and my phone still sleeping in its rice box, and the job that I have no way of contacting, no way of making the cause of my absence known to. All I know is light, soft and warm and spring-like, filtered through the window and onto my face.

The clouds are back, but their anger has gone. They are soft and white, like cotton fibres. And Mark is beside me, breathing softly in his sleep.

I stand up, the morning washing my skin with golden warmth. I close my eyes and imagine myself bathing in it – swimming in it. Then I remember: the lochan! Today we can swim.

I eat breakfast outside, skimmed milk and muesli, the sun straining to warm my back. There's a breeze – I can see it rattling the elm tree – but the garden is a sanctuary. Its tall hedges and walls protect us.

(We are safe here.)

I leaf through the pages of a book. I potter about in the garden, pulling weeds that are newly sprouted, stomping down nettles that cling to the shade. *Silver bells and cockle shells and pretty maids all in a row.* The shadows are bitter cold, deep winter. But the sun says that summer is almost here.

"There you are," Mark says from the patio. He's in just his pyjama bottoms. He rubs his eyes.

"Hello, sleepyhead."

"Is the power back on?"

"The light on the fridge was out. Have you had breakfast?"

"No, not yet."

I walk past him and cup my hand against his shoulder. His skin is warm, and he flinches back slightly. My fingers are tingling with the nettles' sting.

"Have something to eat and then get dressed. I want to walk to the lochan today."

"Today?" Mark is behind me. It's dark in the cottage – so much darker than outside. For a moment I can't see anything, and I have to blink several times before the table, chairs, and the Aga slowly take shape. "Don't you have work?"

"How can I work when the power's out?"

"Won't you get in trouble?"

"It'll come back on tomorrow. I might have to work an evening or two, but that's fine."

"But surely you need to tell someone."

"How? My phone's broken, and yours doesn't get signal."

"We could go to the village... Find a phone..."

I turn to him. Smile. "It's fine, Mark. Stop worrying." Then, washing up my muesli bowl (*icy cold water*), "Why don't you go and find your swimming trunks and a towel?"

The lochan is two miles away. Closer, if you cut across the fields, but I don't want to be caught trespassing again. There's a hill you have to climb over, then a valley to scale. We start our journey through the woodland – the one that leads to the village – and then follow the forest path north.

"This is fun, isn't it?" I say to Mark. It's like we're children again: scouts with a map and compass, trying to find our way back to camp.

"Are you sure this is the right way?" Mark says.

"Yes. It shouldn't be far now."

My stomach rumbles. I should have packed lunch. Maybe there'll be a café, I think hopefully, although I know that there won't be. Besides, we have no money on us.

The pines thin and we see the hill ahead. Atop the crags are fir trees, sparse in patches, dense and dark in others. Up and up we climb, the sun beating and the wind whipping, until – there! "I can see it!"

"What? Where?"

I point through the trees. "There."

He frowns. "You mean we have to walk all the way down again?"

I grin at him and punch his shoulder. "Come on! We're nearly there!"

The lochan is oval and silver. Its slinky back reflects the sky, so much so that I can barely believe it's water at all. It will be like swimming in a mirror: our heads and shoulders in one world, our tummies and limbs plunged into another. I can see now, as the path winds downwards, that there's a wooden jetty jutting out into the tarn. The air is warmer in the valley, the sun trapped by the hillside. There are broken pinecones and needles at our feet.

"What's that?" Mark says.

"What's what?"

"*That.*" He points. His finger hovers in the air, marking nothing. I search the lake for what he's looking at, but whatever it is, I can't see.

"I don't know what you're talking about."

"There. That floating thing above the water."

I squint at the silver: the breezy ripples, the eerie quiet. Then I see it. A scrunched up, mangled thing, some metres above the surface.

"I think it's a balloon."

"A balloon?"

"Yeah, you know. A helium one. It looks half deflated."

"It's not a balloon."

We carry on walking. "What is it then?" I challenge.

"I don't know. It looks like a *bird*."

"It's too still to be a bird," I tell him. "It must be a balloon. Or maybe it's a bag of rubbish that someone's left there."

"A bag of *floating* rubbish?"

"It's probably an illusion. A trick of the light."

Mark mumbles something that I can't hear. We're nearly at the shoreline now. Roots snake their way into water, cracking the earth as they fight to drink. We must be careful not to trip. The surface still looks silver and impenetrable. I think of what could be submerged beneath. Fallen tree trunks, decaying, becoming sludge as they sink into the depths. Branches reaching out like claws – snagging skin – scraping us open, carving us out.

At the edge of the jetty, we set down our bags. There's a plastic crisp wrapper and an empty bottle of beer. No other sign of life. I unravel my towel and shrug off my jumper. My two-piece is on underneath. "Mark? Are you going to change?" But he's standing at the edge of the jetty, squinting, staring at something in the centre of the loch.

"It is a bird," he says.

"What?"

"It is. Come look."

I walk to his side tentatively and stare forwards. He's right. I can see it now. The thing is hovering some feet above the water, floating but not flying. An airborne corpse. I can see from the jolted angles that it must be dead. A wing, folded under its belly. Its head hangs upside down, limp and rotting, beak upturned to the sky. I glance at Mark, who is standing silent and steady. But I can see from the way his jaw is clamped tight that he's nervous. His eyes are hard – they give nothing away.

I wrap my arms around myself. It's cold now that I'm in just my bikini.

"You don't know that it's a bird," I say, though it's clear that he's right.

"How is it floating there?" he asks, and his voice is waif-like, nearly a tremble.

"A trick of the light," I say again, but I'm not fooling anyone.

He continues to stare at it. Unmoving.

"I'll go see," I tell him. I sit down on the edge of the wooden pier and begin to lower myself in.

"No! Rosie, what are you doing?!"

"It's fine." The water is cold around me. Colder than I thought. It swallows my ankles, my knees, my waist. "I'm going to get a closer look."

"You can't swim with that there!" His voice is high and shrill. There's no masking the panic now.

"Don't be ridiculous." I push off from the jetty, the silver swirling around me – only from this angle, it's black. "I'll be back in a sec."

I swim in lazy strokes of front-crawl, head above the water, eyes fixed on the thing ahead. The water is so frigid that my muscles shrink against it. My legs cramp, refusing to move at will. Drops splash against my face, bitingly cold. I have a sudden urge to plunge my head underwater, to numb my brain, to freeze my thoughts. Then my toe bumps against something. A branch? No, it's not sharp enough for that. It felt soft and bloated – like dead fingers. Swollen and fat. I glance behind me. The jetty is already several metres away. I'm nearly in the middle of the lake.

I scull on my back until I'm directly beneath it. The bird hangs, not hovers. I can see that now. Its weight it slumped downwards, gravity tugging at it, trying to drop it into the lochan like an offering. Its skin is pulled tight in places, its feathers forced awry. Its neck is bent backwards, its gullet surrendering to the sun. The black cap of its head is pointed towards me. Its eyes bore soullessly into mine.

I'm treading water, kicking out, struggling to stay afloat. My legs seize and contract. *Go underwater*, I think. *Go. Let go.* I plunge my head under and scull beneath the surface. Then I open my eyes.

A green world. Murky and shadowed. Shapes flitter past in my periphery. Sunlight cuts in front of me. I look down and see my legs, bloated, misshapen, then the dark, dark depths. Fingers, reaching out for me. Branches. *Dead things.* I squeeze my eyes to resurface and then *I can feel it.* It wraps its hand around me, the corpse, the rope. A bird squawks from overhead – a sharp, guttural warning sound. The dead bird, screaming. And dead bodies, pulling me into the deep.

I swim. My arms thrash against the water. My heart hammers against my chest. Water splashes all around me. My neck aches as I strain to keep it up. It would be faster if I put my head down, but I don't. I can't look back into the water. If I do, I'll see them. They'll get me. I'm sure of it.

I reach the end of the jetty. I pull my hands up to grasp at the wood. I try to jump up but I can't lift myself – I can't get out! Mark sees my panic and he reaches for me. He pulls me up. My arms feel like they're going to click out of their sockets. My tummy scrapes across the wood, two-piece lifting, skin scratching in a rash of red. The jetty is sodden where my body lands. I catch my breath – *one, two* – and then sit up.

Mark stares at me in horror. "Are you alright?"

I manage to nod. "Fine."

"What happened out there?"

I clamp my teeth together to stop myself from shivering. I need to get my towel, and Mark is just standing there, staring at me, looking stupid.

I pick myself up and march towards my clothes.

It takes a while to dress. My fingers are stiff. They won't do as I say. The sun dips beneath a cloud, and for a moment, the air turns cold as December. I pull my trousers on and shudder. Mark just stands there. Why doesn't he help?

When I'm fully clothed, I sit on the edge of the jetty, carefully avoiding the damp. My legs are crossed so that they don't dangle down near the water. After a minute of standing, Mark sits next to me.

"Are you cold?"

"No," I lie.

"Did you see it?"

"What?"

"The bird. Is it really hovering?"

I shake my head. "Look up."

He looks up. Blinks. Then looks back at me. "I don't get what you mean."

"Look," I say again, nodding to it. "The electricity line."

Mark stares forward again, and I can see by his expression that he's spotted it. The thin, black cable hangs above the lochan, covering its width. The poles themselves are half-hidden in trees, but we can see their siblings, further up on the hillside, marking either end of the tarn in their straight, militant line.

"That's so strange," he murmurs. "Why do they come all the way down here? Why not avoid the lake completely?"

I shrug. "Maybe there used to be a hut down here."

"And the bird?" he asks.

"Tangled in a fishing line or something. I reckon some fishermen found it, or maybe even caught it, and slung it out into the lake. Bad luck that it caught on the electricity wire."

We stare up at it together.

"They must have thrown it pretty high," Mark says.

My body gives an involuntary shudder. "Come on. Let's go home."

It's hard not to shiver on the walk back. The storm clouds gather as we reach the woods. I worry that it will rain. Mark offers me his jumper, and twice I refuse, but then eventually I accept. I don't want him to worry about me. He worries enough as it is.

We've been walking for quite some time when we realise the path has changed. Where there should be pine trees, there are only birch, looking thin and skeletal in their wintry bark. They are too close together, too spindly, too dark. The floor beneath them is full of rotten leaves. The path has thinned so much that I'm not sure if it even is a path anymore, or just an animal trail, leading us further from our route home.

"This can't be right. We must have gone the wrong..."

I pull out the map and consult the compass. But the nib is flailing, refusing to settle on any determined point. I straighten out the map and hold it steady.

"You need to stop your hands from shaking," Mark says.

"My hands aren't shaking."

"Yes, they are. Here, let me..."

"They're not shaking! Just give it a minute to settle."

He stands back, biting his lip. I can tell he wants to say something. I can just see it on his face. He's waiting for me to fail.

"Maybe we should just turn back..." he ventures.

"Stop it. There might be a shortcut through here."

But if there is a shortcut, we don't find one. After several minutes, I shove the map back in my bag and we turn back on ourselves, through the spiny trees to the pine.

"Can I check the map?"

"There's no point. The compass isn't working."

Mark is silent for a long time after that. I want to say something to him, but I don't know what. How dark it is, between these trees, even with their branches broken and their leaves long shed. The sun dips in and out of cloud, as though playing a game with us. Blinding bright, then vanished. Blinding bright, then vanished. Why didn't I pack a lunch?

"Is that the main path?" Mark asks.

I glance up. "I don't think so."

The track looks similar, but the trees are different. Larches. I would have noticed before.

Our footsteps beat against the ground like a pulse.

"Can you look at the map again?"

"I told you. The compass isn't working."

"I really think you should check it..."

"It's fine, Mark. We just need to keep walking."

The forest has rearranged itself around us. We, at its epicentre, are the only things that are constant. The trees are shifting, mutating. I can't remember being here before.

I try to judge the time by the height of the sun – and by that logic, can't I judge the direction? But when the clouds disperse, the sky is too white to look at. And when they appear again, the sun seems to have spun on an unseen axis, pointing a different direction to when I last checked.

"Rosie. I think we should turn back."

"We *are* turning back, Mark. We just turned around."

"I really think we should go home now." His voice is bubbling, rising to a hysteria. "Please, Rosie, let's go home."

"We are going home," I tell him, trying to stop myself from snapping. My mind feels numb, like the plunge underwater. Numb, like the blistering white of sky above.

"Rosie, please…"

"Stop!"

I turn around and slap him. *Whack* – just like that. The noise reverberates around us, echoing through the shiver of trees. Somewhere in the distance, a flock of birds caw and flap. My hand is tingling. His cheek is hot.

(*Time fractures. It cuts through us, splitting us in two. I feel it, tingling in my palm as Mark stares at me in horror. We are standing in the garden. We are laughing in bed. Morning sunlight; the darkened forest. We are together, and we're not.*)

Mark stares at me. His hatred is so piercing that I have to look away. His jaw is clamped tight. He is shaking, but not with nerves anymore. He is shaking with fury. Shaking so as not to cry. I want to cry looking at him. My hand hurts so much. My palm is flushed red with blood. And his *cheek* –

I cannot look at him.

"I'm sorry," I mouth, but I can't say it. My throat has closed up. It won't sound the words. Mark has turned and he's walking again. The direction seems meaningless now. How far are we from home?

I trail behind him, and then the tears come. I let them fall in silence. My hand is burning. What have I done? We walk and walk and I'm not cold anymore, but my hair is still wet and my feet begin to ache. We walk and walk until we're finally out of the woods and on the edge of the farmland. Mark leads us home.

"Key?" he says, and I retrieve it from my bag.

"Mark..." I start, crossing the threshold. The syllable sticks against the lump in my throat. But Mark is already out of the kitchen. I count his footsteps, up the stairs. The slam of the door. Then silence.

The electricity is down, but the Aga is still on, slowly guzzling through its tank of gas. I cook dinner and set out two places at the table, but he doesn't come. I light candles in the living room and wait with a pack of cards. He doesn't come.

The light fades through the windows. Is it just me, or are the days getting shorter? Each sunset sooner, surrendering to night?

Midsummer is still more than a month away. Surely that can't be right.

I brush my teeth by candlelight, shadows dancing on the walls. The tap gargles. I spit into the sink. The walls are holding their breath.

Night. Soft darkness and moonlight. Seroquel, sweet, two tablets. The light casts shadows across the duvet. The shapes of buds, of flower and thorn, dance like ripples of water. Underwater we lie here, dreaming, drifting, somewhere between sleep and wake.

101

The day feels sharp and disjointed. Like something smashed and put back together. Shards of glass spilt across a stone floor. I can't think how one thing led into another. I can't see how it happened. Wasn't I so happy this morning? So bright and filled with life?

Mark is so close. I could reach out and touch him, but I don't. The air has taken on a solid state between us: dense, impenetrable. Even as he sleeps, I can feel it. Like a third person squashed into our bedsheets. A phantom cold that clings to us and follows us around.

The wind is weak tonight. The leaves at the window shake in silence. I close my eyes, but I can still feel the branches, shuddering inside my head. *What have I done?*

The silence lasts most of next morning. I go about my day as usual, to the best of my ability. The power is still out. I make coffee on the Aga and peel potatoes, which I'll cook for lunch. Mark comes down for a drink then leaves without word. After breakfast, I work in the garden again, digging holes for bulbs I found in the shed. Tulips, I think, and hyacinths, and other spring-flowers, ready to bloom once summer and winter have passed.

The clouds are back, but the gardening makes for good work, and by the time I've dug up half the flower bed, I feel warm with sweat. My palms are muddy, my fingernails black with dirt. I look up to the rose vine, and I see Mark at the bedroom window, sitting at the sill with his face pressed up against the glass. How pale he looks through pane. His eyes catch mine, and he looks away.

Back to the garden.

Is it my imagination, or were the trees greener before? The first buds of leaf must have blown off with the wind. (Was it really so windy, last night?) Now they have gone back to their bare bones, knobbed and brown, like swollen joints.

I pull up goosegrass, strings of weed and vine. A crow sweeps down from the elm tree. Its neck clicks, and from its gullet it squawks a song. I sing too, an old rhyme as a second bird joins its mate.

> One for sorrow
> Two for mirth
> Three for a funeral
> Four for birth

The crow stops singing, and so do I. Its beady eyes blink at me. It gives another squawk. The weeds stick to my fingers. When I tear them away, it feels like peeling back Velcro. Like shedding a second skin.

> Five for Fortune
> Six for Rue
> Seven for the devil, looking at You

When I lift my head to the vine again, the bedroom window is empty.

No internet, no internet.

My phone being broken makes this a lot more complicated than it should be. I expected the issue to sort itself – for someone to come and fix it, like they would if we were back in the city. But it's been two days now, and I have to wonder: does anyone even know?

I need to find the landlord. He gave me his address when we signed the contract, but I saved it only to my phone. I know where to find him, though.

Upstairs, Mark sits on the bed. He's watching the door, but as soon as I push it open, he turns his back.

"I'm going to talk to the landlord," I say.

Mark says nothing. He shows no sign of having heard me.

"I'll be back by lunch. The potatoes are peeled."

Nothing.

"Well?" I ask. "Are you not even going to say goodbye?"

He leans forward, adjusting his weight. I can hear his mouth open and close, dry, in need of water. Still he says nothing.

I slam the door and march down to the garden. My face feels hot by the time I'm outside. Somehow, I've made things worse. I shouldn't have snapped at him. I know that I shouldn't. There's only one way out of this, if time has taught me anything. Apologise. Beg for forgiveness.

But how can I apologise when he won't even look me in the eye?

I walk away from the cottage, past the woodland and out into the fields. The grass is yellow and overgrown. Nettles and hawthorn; bugloss and briars. Out, past the sycamore tree, across the farmland – trespassing.

I think that the landlord must live at the farm. I've seen the buildings there, on the distant horizon, where the land slopes down then back up again. A long walk, but if I explain why I've come, he'll understand. Then he'll phone an engineer. He might even drive me home.

I carry on walking. By the time the ground begins to decline, I wish I'd brought a bottle of water. I squint at the horizon, searching for the huddle of farm buildings, but I can't see anything. The sky is yellow and hazy. The sun, despite being caught behind cloud, is so bright, my head throbs with it. I haven't been sleeping well (have I said that already?) and I can feel it now. In the pinch of my temples. In the grumble of my stomach. The dry ache of my eyes.

By the time the plain flattens, I'm losing hope. The buildings were right here... Weren't they?

My legs ache from yesterday's hike. I wish that Mark was with me. *Mark*. I can still see the shock in his face when I slapped him. The anger – the betrayal.

How could I do this to him?

I stare at the sprouts of clover at my feet as I walk. How much further? I wonder if I should turn back and head towards the village instead, if I should give up completely, but then something catches my eye. There's a figure, standing at the top of the hill.

My heart lurches. At first, I think it's the landlord. Who else would it be, other than him? There's the jeep, silhouetted against the haze, and a sprightly dog yapping at his feet. But the man doesn't move like the landlord. He's too tall and thin, too gangly. There is something sinister about it. His limbs are like a scarecrow's, limp and clumsy, stuffed with straw. I can hear the dog barking and the landlord (is it the landlord?) shouts at it. Then all of a sudden, he's shouting at *me*.

He's waving his arms, bellowing profanities which scatter with the wind. I start to stride towards him – big, adamant steps – ready to explain. Then he picks up a gun and points it at me.

The gun is long and thin, too. It's the kind you see farmers carry on their way to shoot Sunday game. He's raising it now, with scarecrow arms, level with his eye-line. He stares down the barrel and then *bang*.

The shot echoes around me.

(*The slap of a cheek – my hands pulsing red.*)

I can't see the pellet, but I can see where he's aiming. Right at me. He cocks the gun back, ready to shoot again.

I run. Up the hill, across the fields. My blouse snags against the hedgerows. My boots sink into mud.

By the time I reach the sycamore tree, my stomach is tight with cramp. I bend over, heaving. I think I'm going to be sick. Cold air beats against my lungs. I straighten up, hands shaking, and glance behind me. The fields are empty. I am alone.

I stagger back home, legs taut as I resist breaking into a run again. Relief washes over me when I see the house. That beautiful white painted stone! Mark is in the garden and I rush to his side. "I'm so sorry," I cry, and I *am* crying, real tears. "I'm so sorry."

His hand finds my hair, surprised. He holds me close to him. "What for?" he asks.

I can't summon the energy to explain. I nuzzle my head into his chest and breathe in the smell of his clothes. Soft, warm. *We're safe here*, I tell myself; my mantra. *It's going to be okay.*

Mark gathers me in his arms and hugs me. Then he straightens me up and looks at me, holding my gaze in his with that way he has that makes it impossible to break away.

"Rosie. What happened?"

My stomach clenches. I want to be sick. "The landlord–" I start, but breath fails me. "The landlord, he–"

He rubs my arms. "I'm here," he says. "It's okay. I'm here."

I blink, tears dripping onto my face. My lips taste of salt. I huff out a laugh. How stupid it feels to worry, in our garden, with Mark at my side. I sniff and give a shaky nod.

"Okay," I say. "Let's go inside."

You would think the silence would break after that, and it does begin to. But there is no sudden thaw, no avalanche of apology. Mark still quietly avoids me, treading softly about the house, keeping a careful distance as though I am a fuse waiting to spark. But there is something between us – a supportive smile, a wistful glance – that shifts back into place, and I know that everything will be okay.

It is no use telling Mark about the landlord. I can still see him, in scarecrow form, raising his rifle to shoot. The vision brings with it a fresh wave of terror: hot then cold, like a sweat. My mouth turns dry. My tongue is sour. No, Mark doesn't need to know.

I peel the vegetables. Stir the pot. I wash the board down with cold, soapless water.

After dinner, there is a thud outside.

We're in the living room when we hear it. The sound is dull and flat. I look up at Mark, who is curled at the furthest corner of the sofa, folded into himself so as not to spill onto my side of the cushion. He looks back at me, pupils wide.

"I'll go," I tell him.

The shadows in the kitchen have grown larger in the afternoon hours. A candle flickers underneath a glass – trapped like a spider, scrambling to find a way out. The thud came from the front door.

What if it's the landlord? What if he's waiting for me with a gun, and blows my brains out onto the creamy kitchen walls?

I undo one latch, then the other. The metal is cold. The air tastes of sulphur. I swing open the door, feelings its weight strain against my wrists. There is nothing.

Then I look down.

I almost step on it. That's how close to the threshold it is. Its empty eyes are fixed lifelessly on me. Its black wings are misshapen, its feathers ruched, strung tight.

I look up, wondering where it came from. Then I feel the warm shadow of someone behind me.

"What is it?" Mark asks.

"It's a bird." I move my shoulder so that he can see.

"Where did it come from?"

I glance up at the sky, which is now clouded with storm clouds. There are no perches, no nestings above.

"It must have been on the roof," I say. Then I bend over to scoop it up.

Mark's hand comes down on my shoulder. It's the first time he's touched me since I ran back from the farmland this morning – and besides that, the first time all day. He must recognise this because, not a second later, he flinches away, as though my flesh is searing hot.

"What are you doing?!" he demands.

"Well I can't leave it out here."

"You can't bring it inside!"

I cradle the crumpled thing close to me. Its eyes stare back without emotion.

"It's dead, Rosie. What on earth are you going to do with it?"

"I'll bury it in the morning. Look, it's going to rain."

I push past him, into the kitchen. I can't leave the bird outside. Strange though it might seem, I can't shake the sensation that somebody is watching us. The rooks in the trees, perhaps, or whatever was on that hill. This bird has marked us somehow. It needs to be out of sight.

I lay out pages of newspaper on the table and place the corpse there. Mark is pacing, muttering things about *disease* and *insanity*. I pull the candle closer and lift the glass lantern, freeing the flame. The light dances wildly, stretching tall with the sudden surge of oxygen.

"I'm not going to stand for this," Mark is saying. "I'm not going to sit here with that thing."

"Then don't."

He rocks back on his feet, wavering. He opens his mouth to say something, then clamps it shut. I fetch another tealight from the drawer and hold it against the flame, pretending not to watch him. The wax drips hot against my hands. In my periphery, I see him turn and leave. The door slams a second later.

I put the tealight down and sit at the kitchen table. Outside, thunder clouds fester. They gather so fast, snatching the sun from the sky and drowning it in their inky haze. What is left is a dulled twilight. It seeps through the crack of the door, bringing with it the ethereal air of night-time: the fresh chill, the calls of owls and snuffling animals. Shadows grow against the walls. When they reach the clock, I'm reminded of a sundial; of shadow and sunshine working together to split the day in two. Only now, darkness swallows time greedily. Hours are devoured like seconds. The candles tremble in defiance.

The sounds of the house are amplified in the dark. The human noises of routine, of footsteps creaking against floorboards and brushes bristling against teeth, have long since been quiet. But there are other noises – other shrieks and groans that move through the walls as though the stone is animal. The ticking of pipes which, with no hot water, should not click. The scurrying of mice, of rats, scampering beneath the flooring. The drumming of a moth, trapped in a web at the window. The rose bush – tap, tap, tapping upstairs.

I huddle over the corpse to examine it. Its wings have been bent backwards. The bones feel as though they've snapped. The skin is pulled tight it places, as though it's been suffocated. An image flashes through my mind: the corpse above the tarn – dangling, disfigured. I think of the crow in the Larsen trap. *One for sorrow, two for joy.* An omen, planted on our doorstep.

I draw my fingers away and see they're stained red. The blood is thick and sticky; more like oil than ink. I press down on the body again, feeling its feathers for where they are wet.

There. Something scratches against my finger. It's sharp. I press my finger down and feel it pushing against me like a needle. If I push any harder, it will puncture my skin. Then my blood will spill into the bird and mix, so that it's not clear where I end and death begins.

(I don't.)

I pull my finger back, then pinch at the needle. It catches between my nails. I lift my finger, red, out of the gore to reveal the source of the scratching. It's a wire.

The corpse jolts when I tug the wire, like a puppet on a string. Its limp body shudders and dances as I try to yank the copper thread from its gut. The stench in the air is heady. My stomach rolls with nausea. Has it always been so dark in the room? The windows are refusing to let in light.

I pull.

I see the metal now, entangled with strings of tendon and bone. It's twisted amongst the organs, knotting together gut and lungs. The more I pull, the tighter the knot becomes. The feathers jolt. The vacant eyes stare up, unblinking. Bird has become machine.

My hands are shaking. My shoulders ache from sitting so taut. I scrape the chair backwards, and the sound echoes through the hollow room. I think of the lake, and the cable overhead. Of the bird in the Larsen trap – the farmer with the gun. Where did it come from? Who put it here?

The tealights have nearly melted. The wick struggles, fighting for air.

I need to light more candles.

Upstairs, Mark paces. The sound is steady as a heartbeat. *One, two, three, turn. One, two, three, turn.* I rummage through the drawers for the matches. I place the candles in a circle, like a shrine to the dead. The wicks catch. The light sizzles and sparks, warming my palms.

The heartbeat stops.

Then it picks up again, this time slower. The timbre has changed. He's walking down the stairs – across the hall. His steps are muted as his feet find the carpet.

"Is it gone?"

I shake my head.

"Rosie, please..."

"I'll bury it in the garden." I look up at him, giving him my best smile. "Okay? Nothing to worry about."

My heart is thumping as I say it. I don't want to go out there. I don't want them to see.

Mark folds one arm across him chest, and his hand hovers there, reaching for an invisible itch. "You'll do it tonight?"

I nod, still smiling.

He frowns. "What's wrong?"

I glance to the window. The darkness is gathering, thick. I can't tell him that I'm scared. He'll only worry. That's why we moved here – so that I could protect him.

"I should do it now," I say. "Before it gets too dark to see."

He follows my gaze. "What if it rains?"

"I'll wear a coat."

"Do you want me to come with you?" he asks.

"No."

Outside, the wind roars. My hair lashes across my eyes. I struggle to hold it back. The bird feels too light to have once lived. I hold it by its feet, with its head thrown down and eyes watching Mark in the doorway. He is watching the bird and the bird is watching him.

I walk into the darkness.

I can hear the wings rustling in the trees above. They are watching. I know they are. I try my best to walk steady. I resist the urge to look up.

There's a shovel next to the shed. I pick it up and start to dig. The ground is hard and stiff. Too hard – it feels as though it's tight with frost. The hedgerows shiver. The elm creaks. I dig the sole of my foot onto the shovel, forcing the earth to crack.

The burial is hasty. I use my hands to trowel the dirt over the body. Somehow the spade feels too impersonal. All the while, I'm glancing over my shoulder, half-expecting the landlord to be towering over me with that dog gnashing at his ankles. I plant the shovel back in the earth and turn back towards the house.

Mark is still standing in the doorway. The candlelight dances behind him, making the kitchen look like an eerie otherworld of fire.

"The lights aren't on still," he says. Does he really think I've failed to notice?

"I'll ring for someone in the morning."

He follows me upstairs, close as a shadow.

"My phone still won't get signal. I keep trying, but it just won't work."

"I'll walk to the village then."

In the bathroom, I turn on the tap. It creaks, then gushes. The water's ice cold. I dip my knuckles into the basin and scrub. My nails are black with dirt and blood.

I open the cabinet. *Duloxetine. Seroquel.*

"Are you mad at me?"

I slam the case shut.

"No."

He's playing a game with us, I think as we lie in bed. The landlord must have brought us here just to play a game.

Did he plant the Larsen trap? Was it put there as a test?

I roll onto my side.

He strung the bird above the lochan. Who else would have walked there at this time of year?

A game – like the salmon-wrapped cardboard that rots in the corner of the closet, with its sinister-faced clock and its blunted silver pieces. One step forwards, two steps back.

Did he draw us here especially? Who else is in on the joke?

I close my eyes and see the crow cut open. Where its guts should be, there are cogs and broken clockwork. Its veins are made of wire. Its throat is a piston, its heart a dead battery. The rooks in the trees are spying on us. The rose must be in on it too, tap, tap, tapping against the window like the endless whir of a machine.

And then I remember the agency website. An accident, they'd said.

What happened to the people who lay in this bed before us? Does their life still stir in the dust upon the mantle? Do we breathe in their used air?

I wish I could switch off my brain.

We have moved into a different age. Time is slower without the washing machine; without the Aga. I pile our clothes into a mop bucket and soak them in cold, soapy water. I scrub until my hands are scraped raw. Mark makes a fire in the lounge. The chimney was full of cobwebs and wasp nests. He had to crawl into its mouth with his feet wedged against the brick. His knees buckled and clumps of soot stuck to his eyes, but I insisted. I will do what is right for us, no matter what it takes.

I pile the damp laundry into a basket, and step outside. Right away, my spine prickles with unease. The birds are watching me. I can feel them. Their eyes follow me from dawn until dusk. Did they see me bury their friend last night? Is that why they won't leave me alone? I'm hanging the first shirts on the line when the rooks come into the trees. They come in a swarm. A murder of them – or is that crows?

They are chattering so loudly, I can barely hear myself think. I grab at the washing: a pillowcase, a cotton t-shirt. Mark's socks, still damp at the toe. I imagine them covered in droppings. Of me, covered in droppings, turned to stone like a cemetery angel bleached white in dung. I lose a sock in my haste, and scramble to pick it up. Their screams drum deafeningly against my ears. I want to out-scream them. I stare up at the sky, where the rooks are gathering. They twist, coiling, changing shape. Am I imagining it, or do their shapes have meaning? An arrow. A dagger. A noose.

I run. I hold the washing basket above me, the wicker loops ready to catch their slimy droppings and leave me clean.

Chickenshit, I tell myself.

I reach the door and bolt it shut behind me. Who am I locking it from? It seems like a good idea.

I put the basket down and remember to breathe. Then, at the window, I stare out. The birds have settled in the trees, black and formless. Their chatter has stopped.

There, on the grass, is a straggler. It hops towards me – one hop, two – then jumps onto the window ledge. It stares at me with its glassy eyes. They're the eyes of a doll, stitched in tight. It cocks his head and leans forward. Its beak *taps* against the window in a peck.

The rook is black like a piece on a chess board. A breaching tower, pressed up against a wall.

It knows. I'm not sure what it knows yet, but I know that it does. There is some incomprehensible knowledge trapped behind those eyes; a riddle waiting to unroll; a puzzle for us to crack.

We are under siege.

I can't stay in this house a second longer. We need to get to a telephone. We need to get away.

I drop the laundry basket on the sofa and announce, "We're going to town."

I lead the way to the village with Mark behind me. I can feel that he's struggling to keep up. The air cuts right to my lungs. It's only when we're well into the forest that I allow our pace to slow, and our feet find their regular rhythm between the silence that swells between us.

"It's rained again," Mark says, and he's right. Puddles of mud gather in the track hollows.

I'm not in the mood for talking. My mind is too full, it cannot focus on one thing. As we walk through the woods, the branches above us shake. The lines of pine bend and collapse as we pass them, turning into diamonds and prisms, then flattening. I point to a gap through the rows. "We can cut across that way," I say.

We walk on.

Mark is itching his arm again. I think of his skin covered in blotches, like hives. He should really stop it, I tell him. Otherwise, he'll bleed.

Then he stares up to the trees and says: "The birds are watching us."

I follow his gaze. Crows stare down on us, their eyes black as beetle shells. I feel them pinned to me, like a target. I can hear the cogs whirring in their brains.

"Don't look at them."

Back to our feet.

"The bird last night..." he begins.

"I buried it."

"Where did it come from?"

"I don't know."

A few muffled paces. Splatters of mud cake the grass.

"Did you kill it?" he asks.

"Why would you say that?"

"I'm just asking."

"Why would you even *think* that?"

"You don't have to answer."

My shuffled tread becomes a stomp. The crows above us begin to screech.

"Rosie..."

"Is that really what you think of me?!"

Excited, the birds bristle and shake.

"Of course not. I just..."

"I moved out here for you, Mark. I dropped everything for you."

"I know you did. I'm sorry. I..."

I stop.

"Where's the turning?"

Mark glances around him. "What turning?" He sounds so stupid.

"The turning to the village. We must have missed it."

"We don't turn off this road. It's just straight."

"No, we turn right, then down into the valley."

Why is he being like this?

"Come on. We need to go back."

We walk for what feels like hours. We follow the road – turn back on ourselves – criss-cross between the poplar and pine. The forest has mutated. Multiplied. It's stretched itself out like pastry rolled too thin. The trunks are repeating themselves: tree after tree after tree. My eyes grasp for markings I can track. In the branches above me, a tangle of twigs forms a hive. Have we passed this nest already? But there's another a dozen yards away – then another after that.

The forest has stretched, and we have shrunk.

We keep on walking.

"We must have missed it," Mark says.

"Missed what?"

"The turning."

"I thought you said there was no turning."

He looks at me. He frowns.

"I never said that," he says.

My feet are aching. The sky ahead is drawing out. Light is fading, settling to cobalt blue. There's a chill in the air that wasn't there before. Can it really be night already?

It doesn't add up. My brain throbs as I try to make sense of it. We left not long after breakfast. We can't have been walking all day.

"Let's go back on ourselves," I tell him, but there's no disguising the quiver in my voice. "Maybe it was longer than we thought."

"We should head home," Mark says. "Before it gets dark."

"But it was right *here*. I'm sure of it."

He places a hand on my shoulder. "Come on."

I set out early the next morning. I walk for miles and miles. I count every twist and turn of the track. Each bird's nest. Each broken trunk.

The day after, I follow the road around the woodland. I follow it until the tarmac turns to gravel and the gravel disappears into a thin scattering of stone amongst the barren planes.

There is no village. Trees have grown over it. Or perhaps it never existed at all.

I sit across from Mark at the dinner table, spooning baked beans from a can onto two plates. I set his in front of him and watch as he eats.

We will not make it out of this alive.

How long will the food in the cupboard last? The meat is already beginning to decay. A feast of flies has made its way into the fridge. In the absence of cold, I imagine them gorging themselves fat, buzzing and biting at the flesh until all that remains will be the strings of tendon and crusts of blood against bone.

The beans last night were a mistake. We should eat through the fresh food first. Save the cans for last. Everyone knows that, don't they? It's survival 101. Meats and fresh veg, then bread, then cheese.

How much of this can be cooked? And how much cooking will kill off disease? I'll gather sticks for kindling when the wind stops. It's howling outside. The old Gods are brewing up a storm.

How much longer can we live like this?

"Come to bed," says Mark, and his arms wrap around me. I'm standing in the kitchen, staring at the clock face. Its hands shake, struggling to move forwards. I stare and stare the second hand, which is so thin and brittle that it looks like it might break. I stare so hard that my brain starts to blister, then –

Look.

"It moved backwards! Look Mark, it moved backwards."

"I didn't see anything, Rosie."

Rosie, come to bed.

Tomorrow, I tell myself. Tomorrow I'll walk again to the farm and find the landlord. I'll explain about the power cut. He'll understand.

How many pills do you have left?

Mark shakes the bottle. A single capsule falls into his hand. He swallows it dry, then fills his hand with water and gulps.

I rest a hand on his shoulder. I give it a squeeze. In the mirror, I see our two figures, slightly hazy through the dim light of dusk. Our eyes meet through the reflection and I think about how distant we are from each other; how the world that he carries round in his head is as alien as the shrouded realm of the mirror. He smiles at me glumly. At the window, in the bedroom, the rose trums against the glass.

Where did the village go? And why hasn't the landlord come? When will the power come back on?

Who sent that bird?

The birds are watching us. Their eyes pin to me as I pace the kitchen floor. I bite my lip and hum to distract myself.

Sing a song of sixpence, a pocket full of rye.

I see their shadows as they flock in the elm tree.

Four and twenty blackbirds, baked in a pie.

We shouldn't have moved here. There's a curse over this house. A pestilence. All who dwell here will lose their minds. I think of the couple that lived here before us. Did they pace this room in search of an answer? Did they lose the village – the farm – the landlord?

I see him, in my mind's eye, marching down the hillside towards me. There's a gun in his hand. He was trying to warn me. No –

He is watching me.

It's a trap. A snare. I'm a bird inside a cage, but for what purpose? For cruelty? For sport?

The cottage is suffocating. There's not enough air to breathe. It smells as though something has died in here and is rotting. The stench of clotted blood and mangled decay rises, thickening.

My throat burns with acid. I cough and splutter into the sink. I dry heave, but nothing comes up.

"We shouldn't have moved here," I mutter to myself. A crow is perched on the windowsill. It stares at me. It blinks. "We shouldn't have moved here!" I scream. The bird flaps its wings in panic and flies away.

"What's wrong?" Mark asks.

I spin on my foot to look at him. His face is so placid. His voice is almost *taunting* in its calm. As though there's nothing to be worried about. This is the problem. I shield him from everything. I'm the dam, holding back a storm. But while I'm risking everything to shelter him, battered and wind-torn, bruised and exhausted, he's fucking clueless.

"What do you mean, *what's wrong*? We're going to die out here! We're going to fucking die!"

"Hey, hey. Calm down. It's just a spot of bad weather. The power will be back soon."

How can he be so stupid? I wish I was like him; pathetically hopeful and naïve. Doesn't he see what's happening to us?

"We need to go home."

"This *is* home, Rosie."

"We need to go back to the city."

His hands are on me, trying to placate me, but I shrug him off.

He's staring at me, looking shocked and stupid. Like *I'm* the crazy one. Like it's *my* fault that we're here.

"Are you just going to stand there?" I demand. "Aren't you going to do anything?"

He looks me up and down. How can he be so calm?

"Have you taken your medication today?" he asks.

My mouth is dry. I want to scream.

"I moved here for you." I pronounce every syllable. "I did *everything* for you."

"It doesn't matter about the power. We'll call on the landlord in the morning."

"You don't understand—"

"Calm down Rosie."

He tries to grasp my wrists but I won't let him. I squirm away. How can he talk to me like this, after everything I've done? I changed jobs; I left my home. And now he wants to go to the *landlord* – as if he will magically fix all our problems. As if we can even contact him without

124

a phone! Does he not see that we're trapped here? How can he not see what's going on?

His eyes are large and doleful. I don't want him to be sad. *Look at me!* I will him, trying to catch his eye. But he stares sulkily at the floor, like an ungrateful child. Doesn't he want this life I've made for us?

"I'm just trying to make you happy," I tell him. I clasp my hands on his shoulders, forcing him to look me in the eye. "Why can't you see that I'm trying to help you?"

"Rosie..."

"What?"

I'll get us through this. I'll keep you safe.

"You're hurting me."

My fingers grip into his flesh. I can feel his skin under my nails. But he doesn't understand. I have to hold him tight, so that I can hold him together. I'm doing this for him.

"*Rosie.*"

He's shaking. I can see the tears welling in his eyes – his bottom lip trembling as though he's going to fall apart. He's hysterical!

"Don't break down," I tell him. "Don't do this. We need to stay strong."

"Please, I said it doesn't matter about the power. I'm not mad at you."

He's talking nonsense. He's high-strung with stress. I need to make him calm. I need to keep him safe.

He wriggles underneath me, but my grasp stiffens on his shoulders. I wish he wouldn't make me fight him. Doesn't he see how hard I'm trying?

It all happens so quickly. One second, I'm in control – the next I am not. His shoulders slip from my grasp. He tackles me, fingers clutching round my wrists, trying to restrain me. I tussle, struggling to pull away. Is he hurting me? It's too fast to tell.

He reaches for my arms again. I flail. My hands thrash at the air. He's out of control! Now I'm hyperventilating. There's not enough breath in the room. I don't want to panic, but he's making me. I need to stay in control – I need to help him.

"Rosie, will you just *stop*–"

I shove my weight against him. I'm trying to hug him – to hold him – to make him stop. His head crashes against the plaster. His eyes open wide. His fingers twitch around my wrists, and then they go limp.

Mark slouches forward and I stumble back, shrugging away from him. His body slips and sways, and I have to lurch to catch him as he falls to the ground. My hand is on his head, hot and sticky with sweat. No, not sweat. Blood. I can see the blood now. It's smeared down the walls in a pinkish streak; all the way from the clock to the skirting board. It leaks from his hair like oil. The back of his skull has cracked open and his life spills out onto the mud-stained carpet.

I listen for breathing, but there is none.

IV
ASCENDANCE

How much of our minds are made of darkness? The gaps between knowledge and impulse. The blank, vacant spaces between neurons and cells. The empty feats of nothing that hang from each thought.

We wake in the dark. (I wake. Mark is still asleep.) The sun should have risen already – I am almost sure. But my laptop battery has drained itself empty. Our phones have long-since died. The clock in the kitchen points to '5', as it has since yesterday evening. There are no timekeepers for us to turn to but the growing light, half-hidden in the overcast sky. There is no calendar but our bodies, counting down in their gradual decay.

Light creeps across the staircase. It crawls onto the tabletops, catching the milky wax of the candles, now blown cold. The house is eerily quiet.

I ignore the pool of dried blood, matting the fibres of the carpet. I don't give notice to the smear of pink on the wall. If I gather wood and dry it out, I can make a fire. I can boil water to make hot tea. Mark will like that. He feels so cold.

My cheeks are stained and salty as if I've been crying. My throat and nose, too, feel hoarse and blocked. Did I cry through the night? I dreamt that I did. I dreamt that Mark was trapped beneath a dark lake, but the water was too deep. I couldn't reach him. I dreamt that we'd been stuck in this house for a thousand years; that thorns had grown through the windows and the walls were choked by vines. I walked through the empty rooms trying to find him – but all I found was shadow and dust.

In the bathroom, the tap is empty. I wrench the metal so that the pipes open. I wait. Has the water gone now, too? Then it splutters and coughs. An icy stream spits into the sink. I run my hands underneath it. I splash my face. From the cabinet, I find Duloxetine. Propranolol, Seroquel. I shake the cartons, but they're empty now.

To the garden. I'll collect firewood. The dawn outside is growing. I see the skies beyond the elm tree glowing with faint light.

One, two, buckle my shoe.
Three, four, unlock the door.
Five, six, pick up sticks.
Seven, eight –

I march across the garden. The light outside is brighter than I thought. My eyes aren't used to it. I have to squint. A sharp wind sweeps through me. It rattles against my soul. Outside, I feel naked. Unprotected. And suddenly, I remember.

Red rinses through me. The memory is *visceral.* I feel it in the pit of my stomach. I can smell it: the smell of flesh and rot and human decay.

I feel the *crack* as Mark hits the wall. The house shaking; the vacant shock in his eyes. I feel his body slump limp against me. If I narrow in on that moment, I can pinpoint the instant at which life left him: the instant when he stopped being Mark and became a bag of muscle and bone zipped up in a skin pouch.

I feel my fingers sticking together with blood. I feel it in my nostrils, fiery, acrid. I *feel* it, *feel* it, *feel* it, like a scream inside of me, tearing its way out.

The keening erupts from my chest. I drop to my knees and cry. My kneecap scrapes against a rock and splits open. I scream until my lungs ache and my throat is dry. I scream, but it's still inside of me, like a poison in my blood.

I drop the firewood I've collected – three lousy sticks that would barely feed a flame. I push myself up with muddy palms. I run towards the house.

Inside, everything is still and silent. I can barely control my breathing, which is frantic and shallow and loud. *He can't be dead,* I tell myself. *He can't be dead.*

My heartbeat rises to my throat. It's choking. I can feel it thud throughout me, reminding me of how hollow I am. The air is stiff and lifeless. I rush through the living room and up the stairs. My feet are moving so fast, I nearly trip over myself. My lungs snatch a gust of something acrid. I reach the bedroom. The door is ajar.

I can't look. I squeeze my eyes shut and count my heartbeats. *One. Two.* Slowly, I peel them open.

The room is quiet. The light, filtered through the windowpane, is soft. Shadows dance across the bed from the leaves of the rosebush. The sheets are streaked blue and yellow, just as they were at dawn, and in the duvet is Mark. He lies in a violent pool of burgundy. There are ugly clumps of brown in his hair, though the pillows are arranged to hide the worst of it. I am ready to scream, but staring at him, my breath catches. There is something so calm about his face, I cannot bring myself to cry now.

I crawl into the bed next to him. I pull the blankets over our legs. I must've left him uncovered when I went out. His skin feels so cold.

I rest my head in the duvet. Is that his breathing, or mine? I try to hold my breath so that I can hear him. I try to watch for his chest to rise and fall. He looks so peaceful when he sleeps. I don't want to wake him.

Sometime between midmorning and the high sun, I fall asleep. When I wake, the room is bright and my head is groggy. I roll over, leaving Mark to rest. What was I doing, I ask myself? My stomach rumbles and I remember. Collecting firewood. Then I can light the stove and cook something to eat.

Trancelike, I walk downstairs.

Red stain on the wall.

White wax, leaking onto the table.

I open the door to the midday sun. It moves across the sky above me, marking the house with its shadow. It cuts the world in two. One side is dark – empty. The other is splintering with life.

Out into the open.

Bending down, I gather the twigs. The earth shifts underfoot. Branches snap. I feel the rough bark coarse against my fingers. I think of the fire I'll light. What meal will I cook for Mark?

Mark.

Terror grips me. It washes over me again – the red memories, flushing hot through my blood, then draining the life out of me, leaving my cheeks pale and my brain cold. I rush back into the house – past the kitchen – up the stairs. But when I'm there, it's as though *outside* never happened, and all I can think of is calm. *He's only sleeping,* I tell myself. *He'll be okay.*

On and on it goes. I drift through the day as though it is a dream. I burn balls of newspaper in the grate. They burst into flames, wilt and crumple. Their short-lived warmth thaws my hands. I hum songs to break the silence. I eat baked beans from a can.

In moments of clarity, I am there again, in the hallway last night. It's like time has fractured, and I am ripped in two. I walk and breathe in the present, but my mind drags me back into the past.

Outside, the birds gather with the dusk. They flock to the trees in mass, bringing with them the air of mourning. I watch as they shroud the branches like a cloak. They are the veil, closing over us, sealing our fate.

I kneel by the bedside. I scream.

Won't you say something to stop this? Won't you do something? Move? Breathe? Anything?

I watch as the sky turns dark. Has the house always been so silent? I feel as though I'm the last living thing on earth.

Then, the rose taps against the window. If I close my eyes, I can mistake it for a heartbeat.

So I close my eyes and dream.

Day and night run into each other – like two cups poured into the same bowl. Wake and sleep, tangled together, so that I don't know what is real. Moonlight and shadow dance amongst us. My breath is cold against the night. We lie here, silent, as threads of thought lace together. A web of knowing winds around me. The horror of it is no longer fresh and tender. It feels distant – dulled – like skin that's been numbed by icy water. You're gone. I know this. I am alone.

For two days, I lie there. The light shrinks and grows. Outside, clouds glow red then pink then gold. The feverish blaze of dawn burns and withers, leaving a wash of blue in its wake.

Wake. Like the crest of a wave and the bubbling strew of foam it leaves behind. The aftermath. The things we give up – abandon – left to crumble and fall to the ground.

People wake. They wake up from sleeping. They stir. They come to life. They wake suddenly to a blinding revelation, after living for years in the dark.

You can hold a wake, too. Not in your hand – but in your house, perhaps. You go to a wake dressed in black. You say a vigil. You remember. How bitterly cruel to hold a wake for those who will forever sleep.

So. I am awake.

136

I sit up. My back aches from lying. The air is stagnant, like a pond filling with algae. The stench has leaked into the mattress. It's choking.

Night has become day and day become night. I have lain watching the darkened skies outside my window, and I've fallen asleep as the sun comes up. Time is a knot that has loosened. I am no longer in its grasp.

Downstairs, the kitchen is arctic. My breath is white against the air. And outside, the ground is frozen with frost.

Has winter come already? The branches are completely bare. The days are shorter. There's more darkness than light. Did I sleep throughout the whole of summer, and autumn too? But no – everything is just as I left it. Only, the water is now stiff in the taps. The grass is frigid with a coat of ice. Time is moving backwards.

How long until someone looks for us? There's food to last a week – maybe two, if I can get enough wood to keep the fire going. Does the landlord even know we're here? Perhaps we haven't arrived yet. Perhaps this is all a dream.

Downstairs, there is a knock.

I rush to the window, heart racing for joy. But when I see the jeep outside, and the moss-green jacket, I'm numb as ice.

The landlord raps at the door, then crosses to the kitchen window to peer inside. I retreat into the shadows, watching the dog silently yap from the windscreen of the jeep. My spine is taut as I wait for the knocking to cease. It jars in a menace: *knock, knock*, then silence. *Knock, knock*, then silence. I long for someone to find us, but not him. Not now.

Mark is rigid beside me. He must be frozen with fear. Suddenly, the only thing worse than not being found is being found by him.

Does he have a key, I think? Will he turn the lock open and bleach the kitchen in ugly light? Will he walk past the pink smear on the plaster, the dried pool of red that has seeped through the carpet, into the wooden boards? What will he do to Mark when he finds us? What will he do to me?

The door shakes. The house trembles in resistance. I stand frozen until the knocking subsides. It feels like an eternity. Then finally I hear the growl of the jeep rising and the stone path rattle as it's churned to dust. Only then do I creep forward to watch the vehicle plough its way across the farmland.

When my heart has settled, I tiptoe downstairs. I stand in the doorway, staring at the kitchen. Rammed through the letterbox is a note.

Slowly, I cross the room to open it. The landlord's scrawly hand reads:

> *Tree fell on track last week. Road blocked, power out. Tried to contact you. Electrician coming soon.*

I stare and stare and stare at the words. *Road blocked*, he says. *Power out.* But I walked down that road mere days ago. There was no tree to be seen. A sinister sense curdles in my stomach. He is trying to trick us. He wants us trapped here.

Road blocked.

I rush outside. The wind whips against me as I march down the road. It threatens to blow me over, but I carry on. I follow the track to the edge of woodland, where the strings of cable disappear between the trees.

Power out.

Did he cut the electricity lines? Did he summon the storm? I picture him like a vengeful God. He stands on the hill, unyielding to the wind. He raises a gun to shoot.

Tried to contact you.

(And did he really shoot at me? Or was that just in my head? I haven't slept in such a long time, and I'm beginning to see shapes in the darkness. There are faces in the knots of trees, and phantoms form from the blurred shadows of my periphery. Did I see a face in the window, on the ladder? Did my mind give voice to the crow?)

A tree fell on the track last week, but now it's nowhere to be seen.

The crows are still gathered in the trees. I can't shake the feeling that they're watching me. For all I know, they are made of wires, recording our every move. Which is more likely, I wonder? That there are separate souls in every body, clinging to every ounce of flesh, breathing thought into blood and nerve and muscle? Or that I am alone here: a vessel who, by miracle or accident, stumbled upon the curse of conscious life? I walk to the shed where I find an axe. Then, weapon in hand, I march towards the woods.

A flock of rooks take flight as I pass beneath them. They squawk and cry as their wings lift to the sky. I keep walking, through to the gloomy wood. It doesn't take long to find a fallen tree. The winds are wild here. It's a treacherous, unforgiving place. I swing the axe and begin to chop. As the wood splits, I sing.

Who killed Mark?
I, said the Crow
With arrow and a bow
I killed Mark.

Who saw him die?

I, said the Fly.
I saw him die.
Who'll barter with above?

I, said the Dove.
I mourn for my love.
What will I do?

He's looking at You.

My voice catches in my throat. Beads of sweat collect on my forehead. It's eerie in the woods. I'm suddenly aware of it. My hands are cold as ice, but my neck and scalp are hot to touch. I hear the leaves rustle. Branches snap. Above me, the tree creaks and whines. Its body sways drunk – once, twice – then it begins to fall.

I stand back and watch as it crashes down. Its huge limbs catch on the telephone wire which strings its way to the village at my right. The branches fall: twigs and wire and dead leaves entwined. The trunk thuds across the track, dividing the woods like the gate of a fortress. I gather the logs and rush home.

Inside, I build a fire. I rub sticks together until they spark. There are only a few matches left – best save them until we need them. It takes a while, but eventually the flames catch, and the bark of the kindling begins to sizzle and burn.

I light candles and take them upstairs. I put them around your body.

On the ledge outside, a rook is cawing. Its screech is perilous. I open the window and flap my arms at it, but it won't scare away.

The bird cocks its head at me. "Who killed Mark?" it asks. It cheeps and trills, then bristles its feathers. "Who killed Mark?" it asks again.

Its voice triggers something electric inside of me. It makes me hot and angry and sick. I reach forwards and grab the thing around its neck.

"Mark!" it cries, flapping its wings in a desperate attempt to flee. "Mark! Mark! Who killed Mark!"

I close my eyes and *twist*.

I count the seconds. I can feel its neck bleating with a frantic pulse. Its wings twitch, once, twice. Its claws scratch lazily on my hand. Then the body is limp and silent. Its blood cools quickly, and I feel its muscles turn stiff.

I release the body and stare at the bird. Its eyes are frozen wide in an unreadable expression. I try to gauge what it might have felt. Fear? Anger? Surprise? But there is no clue. Its black eyes are a mirror, throwing back at me my own face. If there ever was a soul, it is gone now.

The branches in the garden rustle. The birds have seen me – they know what I have done. Hastily, I pull the rook inside and latch the window shut.

The food stores will run out soon. It's good to have extra meat.

I find some chicken wire and begin to lace it through the bird's stomach. Once –

One for sorrow

Twice –

Two for mirth

I latch the wire to a hook on the ceiling, watching the corpse swing slowly. With a tug, the bird's lurches as though it's flying. The meat will dry out like a jerky.

I pull apart the wings of rook and string them up high.

Four and twenty blackbirds, baked in a pie.

It swings like a talisman. Like a pendulum, slowly ticking from a clock. I see the other birds flocking at the window. A murder of them, in funeral procession.

Grimly, an idea comes to me. I have no idea how long we will be stuck here. I should do it now, while they're close. While I still have the strength.

For Mark, I think. *To keep him safe.*

It is not a task for the faint-hearted. I have never been good with blood. I try to work monotonously, imagining myself as a cog in a larger wheel. I strike the birds with whatever I can find – a wooden spoon, a frying pan. I avoid anything sharp as the thought makes me squeamish. It's harder than I'd thought. Rooks and crows are clever things. They jump away from sudden movement. They take flight in a herd, moving as one. But there are enough of them that they can't all escape. The chaos works to my advantage. In their confusion as they try to flee, I knock two birds to the ground.

I wait until they're in the trees again before I leave the house. I skulk to the patio where their bodies lie. Glancing over my shoulder, I scoop them up and take them inside.

I work quickly, looping wire around their chests and hanging them up around the house. The chore is not pleasant, but it gives me focus. It calms my nerves. When I'm working, I do not go upstairs. When I'm working, I find I can forget.

So my collection grows.

Sometimes the birds come to me, and sometimes I go to them. In the trees above, I hear them singing to each other. Chattering. In their voices, I hear snatches of conversation.

"My hands aren't shaking."

"Do you want to check the windows upstairs are locked?"

"Are you busy?"

"They make you feel groggy if you take them too often."

Sometimes the work is already done for me. I find a bird dead on the ground with its mouth ajar, its black eyes wide and hollow, its matted feathers beginning to come loose. I imagine another girl roaming the forest. She looks like me, but she's thin and ghostly. She throws rocks at the trees and then scurries away.

I sling the corpses over my shoulders and return home, like a fox bringing its kill into a den. There, I get to work with the stringing. Birds hang from the ceiling like mobiles in a nursery. They sway when I open a door.

To work.

The more birds I collect, the more meat I'll have. The longer I can stay here. *With you, Mark. I'm doing it for you.*

It becomes an obsession.

Night and day blur together. I light candles when it's too dim outside to see. I wait and wait and wait for summer. For the trees green and victorious. Flowers, gay and vibrant. For one blazing spell of heat. Or if not summer, autumn. The smoky taste of air. The chilling wind and the first winter frost. Blackberries; juniper. Sloe and rowan and mistletoe.

I wait and wait and wait. But summer does not come.

The days are getting shorter. I'm sure of it. The leaves are not falling. How could they? They never reached full bloom. Instead, they curl back into themselves. The tree snatches back the life it gave, like a mother smothering its child.

Time is regressing. A hole has opened in the pit of this house, and we are falling into it. In which room, I wonder? The kitchen? The living room? Under the bathroom sink?

A void. Like a dead star, it swallows space and time. Space, for I can no longer remember the village, the houses, the shops we used to walk to. Time, for we are spiralling into the past.

Tap, tap, tap, says the rose against the window.

I wish I could switch off my brain.

Where is our soul? I wonder, as I watch over your body. If I were to cut from your throat down to your stomach – if I opened your bowel and pulled out your guts – would I see it? Where could it be?

You seem so lifeless now. You never stir. You don't make a sound. Do our souls leave our bodies and wander around while we sleep? Do they travel miles under moonlit skies? Do they ever get tired?

I am stuck in this house; in a purgatory wasteland, caught between life and death. Outside, the world keeps turning. The sky spirals through its cycle of night and day. But here, we are stagnant. There is no past or present. There is only us, and there is now.

I search for you in the pockets of my coat. In the Aga. Under the stairs. I wonder if your spirit slipped out when I wasn't looking; whether it fled to the forest to haunt the trees. But I sense it is not so. You are still here somewhere, in this house, with me. And so I trap us here. I won't let you leave.

The windows and doors are shut now. The air becomes still. I've pulled down an old piece of telephone wire. I string up the birds along it like dreamcatchers. They are empty shells; vessels. I pray one of them will catch your soul.

Downstairs, I've gathered the tins and morsels of food. I ration each day. Hunger is familiar now, it seems strange to think it hasn't always been this way. I spend most of my time in bed. I need to save my strength.

My muscles ache if I don't move for too long. I wonder how you manage to do it. I alternate sleeping head and toe, curling up beside you, then moving as far as I can away. My back is stiff from the cold. The last fire died long ago.

I'll have to eat the birds soon. Last night, I crept downstairs and pulled one down from its thread. But when I tore it open to see its flesh, I saw that it was filled with cables and wire. The cord it hung from had multiplied. Metal had planted roots in the skin and claimed the bird as its own. Its feathers buzzed with static. Its eyes were vacant as a camera lens. Then another thought occurred to me – that there are no living things left, only spies. I hurried back to bed, where I am safe.

I think I might be losing my mind.

A smell has begun to fester in the bedroom. I can't leave you there. I lug your body down to the cellar, where it's cold. It's dark down here, but there's a small window with a crack of light. Through it I can see the ugly stem of the rosebush. Its leaves shiver against the glass. There is no escape from them.

I collect the candles and place them around your head. Some of the wicks have burnt out already; others have drowned themselves in wax. I light what is left.

I pluck black feathers from the corpses and spread them between the flames. I make trinkets from wires. I weave charms out of bone. At night, my spirit rises from my body to dance with yours. They tangle together, slipping through the strings I've hung. They spin spider webs against the windows. They sing lullabies to the dark.

There is somebody in the house. I hear them when I try to sleep. They move and alter things around the room – a misplaced sweater, a candle snubbed out. But I do not see them.

I wait in the basement, with Mark at my side. His grey skin has sunk into the stone tiling. At night, it's hard to know where he ends and the ground begins. I think about how our bodies are stitched from the same atoms that make up everything else. How, when we rot, our flesh will be ground down into earth, and bones become dust. We'll be split, ripped apart, and reformed in a million different places. We are recycled like old tin cans.

Sometimes, I hear a girl shouting. Sometimes I hear her cry. Then her cries become squawks, and the squawks are joined by a chorus of wings.

One morning, when I'm upstairs in the bedroom, the sun is blazing in its wintry glory, there's a bump against the window. It thuds, like metal knocking against wood. In the garden below, I hear muffled voices.

"Do you want me to hold it steady?"

"Yes, okay."

I pull myself up on the bed and crane my neck to see. Everything takes effort now. My body is worn and tired. I hear the thud of boots approaching. Like someone climbing a ladder. *They've found us,* I think. Somebody from the village. *They've come to save us.*

I lean towards the window and see –

A raven, with its grey beak open wide, is hovering outside the window. Its great wings flap, levitating. Its eyes bore into me as it clicks its tongue. A thud-like sound escapes it; the sound I thought belonged to a foot. It smacks its beak and tongue together, its throat vibrating to mimic the creaks and groans of metal and wood. It is staring at me. *Mocking* me.

"Rosie?" it says. Its voice feels like a stab to the heart. In spite of myself, a laugh escapes me. I grin manically, laughing until my throat is dry. There is nobody at the window, I realise. There is nobody in this house. It's only the birds. They are an echo-chamber. A mirror, reflecting back on us what we've said before. There is nobody coming to save us. We are alone.

I know that I have killed you. At times, it's blindingly clear. I pray that someone will find me. But if they come, they'll take you away from me. If they come, they'll tear us apart.

I won't let them find us. I love you too much.

My dreams are becoming vivid. Their colours are brighter than in waking life. The sound of the car feels like an earthquake after the silence. The gravel rumbles. A door clicks shut.

I try to lift myself from the ground, but my back is stiff from sleeping on the cellar floor. My arms feel like they're weighed down with stones. The life has been drained out of me and I can no longer bring myself to stand. I feel like a corpse, trying to summon myself from the dead.

I hear the gruff voice, and with a jolt of anxiety, I find I recognise it. It's the landlord. "Will be a pain walking about when the snow sets in," he says.

His voice drifts in from the garden. He's talking to someone else. I catch the muffled reply: "We like walking."

I pull myself up. Every part of my body aches, but I am desperate. I need to see them – I need to know this is real.

I hobble up the stairs to the ground floor – then another flight to our bed. I cross to the window, where the stark light is amplified through the glass.

"Want me to show you inside?"

The latch catches below me. I peer out.

Their voices are louder now. There! I see them! They are real! The girl is nervous-looking and dressed in a sweater. She's pretty, but sallow-looking and scared. There's a man with her. Her boyfriend, perhaps?

"The agency mentioned there was an accident here," the girl's saying. "We just wanted to know a bit more about what happened?"

"Accident is a funny way of putting it," the landlord replies. "Though there's nothing wrong with the house itself, if that's what you're worried about. Living out here... It's not for everyone."

Just then, the boy looks up. His eyes meet mine, and I freeze. It's Mark. He looks just like Mark.

I stare, dumbfounded, at the trio below. The girl clings to him anxiously. The landlord seems hesitant as he addresses her. And Mark, beautiful Mark, tears his eyes away from me. The figures are lost amongst the rose buds. I hear the door click. They are inside.

The house is silent now. Outside, winter deepens in her navy greys. The ground turns hard with frost. I barely sleep. I do not eat. The house has wrapped its spell around us, like a spider snaring a fly.

I have a dream for us, I whisper to Mark as the rose thorns trum against the window and the moonlight swallows us in the tomb. I dream that the garden is blooming, the flowers bursting out of their buds, plum-flesh splitting out from their damson jackets, the rose petals round and swollen, barely clinging to their stems. The sunlight pours in. It catches us, turning skin to gold, teeming warmth upon the white, crisp sheets. My hair is sprawled out like wildflower.

We hold each other – wrist around arm, ankle on leg – as though we're made of vines.

I dream that you turn to me. Your eyes are wide and earnest. No need for thanks or apologies; all formalities have been swept away, carried off with the winds of spring. We lie in warmth, bare, unguarded, breathing in midmorning air.

You're so happy, I whisper to Mark, and I watch as his breath catches and his eyelids flutter with sleep.

You're so happy.

One day soon.

About the Author

Ellen Taylor grew up near King's Lynn, Norfolk.
She studied at York St John University,
Durham University, and St John's College,
Oxford. She currently teaches Psychology at
University of Nottingham.

Said the Crow is her first novella.

Milton Keynes UK
Ingram Content Group UK Ltd.
UKHW041644061223
433896UK00014B/181